MOONLIT FEATHERS

SARAH MÄKELÄ

KISSA PRESS LLC

MOONLIT FEATHERS

After faced with crippling loss, a heartbroken raven must find her wings again...

Treasure hunters are trained to find things, but all Morgana has known is loss. When someone she loves dies because she can't protect them, she shies away from the world, too afraid to let anyone else get close. That won't last long because ravens aren't ones to pass up on shiny things.

Cody has never really felt accepted. He's a coyote shifter of Native American heritage, but he gets his looks from his Scandinavian mother, unlike his siblings and the rest of his people. That makes him all the more dedicated when what seemed like a freak tornado becomes something much scarier.

When Cody realizes that his family's powerful talisman has slips into the wrong hands, he desperately needs help. But he never imagined he'd be fall head over heels for the beautiful, if not, mysterious treasure hunter. Morgana will need to let go of being hurt again if they have any hope of saving not only each other, but also the small town that they both love from disaster.

Sign up for Sarah's newsletter for her latest news, giveaways, excerpts, and much more!
http://bit.ly/SarahMakelaNewsletter

Moonlit Feathers © 2015 Sarah Mäkelä

This is a work of fiction. Names, characters, places, and incidents are either products of the author's imagination or used fictitiously. Any resemblance to actual events, locales, business establishments, or people, living or dead, is entirely coincidental.

Editor: Word Vagabond

Cover Artist: J.M. Rising Horse Creations

ISBN-13: 978-1-942873-81-5

1

MORGANA

Wind caressed my midnight black feathers as I sailed through the early evening sky. Flying had always been a welcome reprieve, an escape from the everyday life of walking on two legs. Most people in the world only dreamed of this gift I'd been granted, but it didn't give me that much freedom from life's sorrows. Perhaps that was just as well.

My line of work demanded more from me than the average human's physique could handle. That was why my peers regarded me as the best of the best.

As a treasure hunter, people expected me to explore mystical ruins and dodge huge boulders, but my main task was to always be on the lookout for stunning riches that might interest my wealthy clients. What set me apart from the rest was being a Raven shifter. That gave me the ability to get in and out of ancient, mythical locales more quickly and safely than most.

Clients came to me with all sorts of requests. Due to my popularity, I could choose the jobs I wanted and who I wanted to work for, something the few fellow treasure hunters I'd met could only dream of. When we got together, they always asked for my secrets—either to my face or behind my back—but I wasn't willing to share the knowledge of my abilities with them.

Only one person, aside from my parents, had ever gotten close enough to see the true me, and he'd died because I couldn't save him when he needed me the most.

How could I truly be happy with a life spent forever alone, regardless of the mystery and adventure my career afforded me?

Loneliness ached like a gaping hole in my chest. Whatever life I'd known before had dimmed the light, and I merely trudged through the shades of grey with my bruised heart.

Ezra Phillips had been the last person I'd allowed to get close to me. He'd crept past the walls I'd erected around my heart after my parents died and left me all alone in the world. I regretted his death every single day. Life with him had been an exciting journey. We were hunting a rare gem with supposed magical properties together, and I'd tried to convince him that I should go alone since he was only human. The job was dangerous, even for me. He had a way with words and convinced me to let him come along. I mistakenly believed we were indestructible together. Neither of us had been to South America before, and now I never wanted to go back.

I was all alone again. Whoever said it was better to have loved and lost had obviously never felt this kind of gut-wrenching pain.

If anything had come from my relationship with Ezra, it was a determination to harden my heart that much more.

Never again would I let someone in. More pain and loss would be too much to bear. Besides, I had a career in shambles that needed to be rebuilt.

Shaking away my destructive thoughts, I swept my gaze over my surroundings, dragging myself back to the here and now. Breathtaking oranges, reds, and yellows spread out beneath me, helping me remember why I'd chosen Woodland Creek, Indiana as my new home. I'd never been a small-town girl, but that didn't matter much. After Ezra's death, I drew more into myself, and the solitude suited me now.

Above the treetops, the air carried the clean scent of ozone mixed with pine. The strong pull from the ley-lines had called me here like a mystical artery pumping with magic, very much alive with raw, untapped energy churning below the ground. For wizards, it made spellcasting easier, but for the shifters I knew of, it acted like a beacon, calling us together.

Through the thick canopy, I caught sight of something shiny on the forest floor below. I'd flown this path many times on my way home, and rarely had I seen any hikers in this area. Could this object be something valuable? The raven in me wanted to investigate—she liked shiny things—but my human side prepared for disappointment.

Maybe I'd become more jaded than I'd realized, if not downright pessimistic.

Swooping toward the ground, we splayed our wings wide and slowed our descent to get a better look. Just an average section of Running Deer National Forest. It's only distinguishing feature was a large ring of boulders. No one was around, and the area was clear of camping gear and human supplies.

I perched on a sturdy tree limb, and it groaned a little under our weight. While most ravens were about three pounds, I was closer to thirty, approximately the size of a cinereous vulture. Not conspicuous at all, right? But most people didn't look too hard at me. They keep their eyes at ground level, not paying much attention to what goes on above their heads.

The shiny object below beckoned my raven closer, but I couldn't be sure this wasn't some kind of trap. Call me paranoid, but that was the sort of thinking that kept me alive. I didn't see anyone else nearby, though: people, animals, or those in-between. The longer I sat there, the more I felt a heaviness in the air, as if someone had recently thrown a lot of magic around. The sensation nearly made me decide to fly away, but my raven *krawed* at me. She thought I was acting like a coward, and that was definitely *not* me. The thought of the *glimmer* had entered into her mind, and once she was set on something, there was only one way to satisfy her curiosity.

With one final glance around to make certain I was alone, I jumped off my branch, shifting into human form as I fell to the ground. I rolled to take the impact off my legs and stood up straight. My raven flapped her wings beneath my chest, preening at the crazy move. Maybe I wasn't completely alone in the world. I did have my raven. But given the trouble she got me into sometimes, it was hard to decide if that was a blessing or a curse.

The cool October wind caressed my bare skin, drawing out a shiver. Wrapping my arms around me for warmth, I hurried over to the baseball-sized piece of...gold? I dropped to my knees beside it, frowning at the rounded lump. With so many people venturing into Running Deer each year, I highly doubted no one would've seen this before now and not have taken it. It was freaking hard to miss. Something else that struck me was how polished the metal appeared. If it had been buried underground for years, it wouldn't look like someone had professionally cleaned it.

Maybe it was cursed. I didn't need any help in that department. My business had taken a turn for the worse after Ezra's death. For the first time in years, I struggled with money, because hunting for other people's gain felt wrong after I'd lost so much. Despite my best efforts to get over it, my head was still stuck in the past. I'd attempted a few jobs in town, but I hadn't stayed long at any of them. My fear of getting too close to anyone made me keep everyone at arm's length.

Before I knew what I was doing, my hand closed around the smooth, round chunk of gold. It was heavy and solid, but it didn't weigh as much as I'd expected for gold this size. I blinked at it in surprise. It wasn't pyrite—fool's gold. It had the softer edges of true gold, and shone from every angle rather than just a few. But something about it wasn't right. This wasn't like any gold I'd ever come across. As well as being too light, it wasn't malleable enough. More like stone than gold.

My raven *krawed* her disappointment.

If anyone could get to the bottom of this mystery, it would be Kevin. Kevin was a wizard, and he used to be a mutual friend of Ezra and me. He'd helped us a few times when we had questions about anything magical—amulets, gems, or artifacts. He was a solid source of information.

Sighing, I dropped the strange golden ball back to the ground with a thud. "Looks like we'll be in for a long flight."

With a sharp push of energy, the raven stretched out of my skin. Her feathers sprouted from my body like a dark wave, and talons grew from where my fingers had been. We shook our wings, letting out a loud *kraa*. When the shift was over, we stared at the piece of gold, cocking our head to the side, until the raven decided we would be able to hold the ball in our claws.

After a couple tries, we lifted off without dropping it and made our way toward Kevin's house in Old Town.

2

CODY

After a long day of classes at Hastings-Albrecht University, the last place I wanted to be was sitting in the library, studying. My coyote paced beneath the surface of my skin, anxious to be unleashed and prowl around Running Deer, but the universe had a way of giving my plans the middle finger. My professors seemed to have conspired against me by planning quizzes in the majority of my classes tomorrow. That meant I had to sit here and soothe my coyote, even if keeping him in one place was like making a kid with ADHD focus on sorting pins. *So hard.*

My coyote perked our ears to listen in on nearby conversations, not helpful when I'd rather be doing anything else but study. Normally I'd go back to my dorm, but my roommate was having his girlfriend over tonight. Didn't want to go through hearing that again, regardless of how my dopey coyote felt.

The words on the page blurred together, and I took another sip of dark roast coffee from Geek Beans. I didn't know why I bothered, since caffeine didn't affect me like it would a normal human. My coyote's metabolism quickly burned it off. His attention was on everything but my textbook. I growled under my breath, causing the two girls at the next table to look up from their books. Maybe I'd been a little louder than I thought. I smiled, and they went back to their reading.

The coyote backed down the tiniest bit, but not nearly enough. He just turned and focused on another couple of students toward the other side of the room. They spoke in hushed whispers. This time I tried to rein him in, but my coyote held firm, as if he knew something I didn't. It gave me pause.

"Did you hear about what's been going on in the forest? Interesting stuff."

I frowned, my curiosity sufficiently piqued. I certainly hadn't heard about anything strange going on. Then again, with my course load being so heavy right now, I wasn't really up to date on everything.

The guy leaned into his female companion, even as she leaned away, obviously not interested in his advances. "No," she said. "What's going on?"

He leaned that much farther into her, either oblivious or unable to handle rejection...or both. "Strange magic." He made a spooky voice as if trying to scare kids around a campfire.

It achieved what he was going for, though. The thought chilled me.

My grandmother had been experiencing some odd and unsettling feelings recently. She wasn't exactly a full-blown wizard like the Sullivans or the Thomases, two of Woodland Creek's founding families. She was more like a Native American shaman. These feelings didn't happen to her often, but when they did, our family made sure to listen. The last time

she'd felt this unusual tension was before our family home
—which had stood for almost a hundred years and through
countless storms—was hit by a powerful tornado that
ripped through the area.

Many of the artifacts we'd passed down for generations
had been tossed around, some broken, others lost. One of
the more powerful magical talismans was presumed
destroyed, although my grandmother had never accepted
that conclusion. She claimed she would've sensed the power
leaving it.

With all the chaos at the time and the rebuilding afterward, I'd shrugged it off, but there were times when I
wondered if she was right. I'd witnessed the strong magic it
possessed when I was younger, and I doubted even a
tornado would destroy it. Magic had a way of preserving
itself.

I brushed those memories away, refocusing my attention
on the couple's conversation. I'd missed some of it, but from
the disgusted look on the girl's face, I doubted it had been
important.

"I should've known this was just another attempt at
getting into my pants." She pushed to her feet as the guy
reached for her.

"Come on, babe. It's not *only* to get into your pants." He
rose to his feet and lowered his voice again. "I thought you'd
want to check out the creepy area my buddy Rex and Roger
found. Said it was like nothing they'd ever seen before, and
around this place, they've seen things that'd keep you up at
night."

Letting out a harsh sigh, the girl ran her hand through
her pixie-cut sandy brown hair. "Fine. Only if you promise
that we'll come back later before the library closes to keep
studying. Jerk." She murmured the last part under her

breath. Her male companion didn't seem to hear her. He gave her a not-so-subtle smack on the butt before gathering up their textbooks and study materials.

While it might've been nothing, I couldn't forget my grandmother's recent warnings. Just to be safe, I'd follow them and see what was going on. Life had been relatively quiet in the six months since the tornado hit. But if someone had found my family's talisman, I needed to retrieve it before they or any innocent bystanders were hurt. The small wooden carving was way too powerful to remain in the hands of someone who didn't know how to use it, including me.

My studies could wait.

3

MORGANA

Kevin lived far enough away from where I'd been in the heart of the forest that my wings ached from carrying the heavy rock. Needless to say, it had taken a few spills. Its smooth shininess might've gained some dirt and a few new dings, but I couldn't exactly say I cared now. When I got home, I'd be soaking my sore limbs in a hot bubble bath to ease some of the strain.

I dropped the golden ball to the ground near Kevin's porch and *krawed* at the closed door. When he didn't answer, I tapped on it with my thick black beak. Still nothing. Kevin didn't go out often, but maybe he wasn't here? Doubtful. I cocked my head to the side, using my raven's heightened senses to check for him. The faintest sound of a man humming came back to me.

Typical. He was likely in his basement laboratory with his earbuds in again. His laboratory was locked down like a fortress. It used to have small rectangular windows, but he'd had them blocked up after inheriting the place from his parents.

That left one option: knock on the door in human form. It wouldn't be the first time he'd seen me naked, and I did need to talk with him about the find. *Ugh...* I *krawed* again, more out of frustration than in hopes of getting his attention.

Feathers retracted into my body, leaving me cool and naked. My bones and muscles stretched from the two-foot-and-change raven form into my five-foot-six human form. I banged my fist against the door as hard as I could, causing the nearby window to shake in its frame. It wasn't supernatural strength, just determination to get home.

"Kevin!" I shouted.

I pressed my ear to the door to listen again. A string of curses followed the loud clattering of several things dropping. Pain shot through my arm and upper back as I grabbed the gold ball and took a few steps away from the house. I knew the kind of magic Kevin toyed around with, and I didn't want to be in the blast zone. I wasn't stupid.

Besides, he knew I was here now. He'd get to me whenever he was finished averting the disaster he was dealing with.

Ten minutes passed, and I considered knocking again. What if he'd been working on a dangerous potion or spell, and I'd broken his laser-sharp focus? Concern clenched my chest. He could need my help. I stepped toward the door, just as it swung open. My raven shook out her feathers below the surface of my skin and *krawed,* feeling every bit as jumpy at Kevin's sudden appearance as I did.

He towered over me at six foot three, with angry hazel eyes and dark brown hair that stood on end. A scowl creased his brow, and he opened his mouth as if to yell at whoever dared darken his doorstep. When his gaze lowered to me, he froze in place.

Shifters might not think much of nudity, but I doubted wizards were as used to it.

Ezra never could hide his arousal over my human form, so he'd always frowned upon me arriving at Kevin's doorstep naked. He never understood how natural and non-sexual this was for me. Granted, being around humans made it different. So we'd driven to Kevin's when we spent time with him. Now, I didn't really care about pleasantries. This was who I was. As a wizard, I knew he accepted that, even if it was a little out there.

Kevin's mouth dropped open, and he sputtered a few incoherent sounds, totally flummoxed for once. "I... uh... Hello, Morgana." He cleared his throat before stepping away from the doorway to let me in. "Um... Sorry it took a moment to answer the door."

The weight of his gaze descended on my backside as I walked past him, and I glanced over my shoulder to cut him a look.

"It's fine." I set the heavy golden ball on the one clear corner of his kitchen table. The rest of it was filled with pizza boxes and Chinese take-out containers. Before Ezra's passing, he'd been neat and organized to near anal-retentive levels, but from the mess and the dark bags under his eyes, I couldn't help but wonder if we were both still reeling from the loss in our own ways. "I have something I'd like you to take a look at."

He closed the distance between us, but his gaze remained forcibly fixed on my face as if he didn't trust himself not to check me out again. It was understandable. He wasn't used to me walking around like this. I wished I had a change of clothes so we wouldn't feel this uncomfortable around one another, especially since it had been a while since I'd last talked with him. The funeral...

My shoulders slumped forward. Thinking back to it made me want to curl into a ball. *Stop it, Morgana...*

Kevin laid his warm hand on my shoulder and frowned down at me. "You know, I'm here to talk if you ever need it. Not only about work, either." Pulling away, he walked to the couch and grabbed a flannel blanket from the back for me. "You can't keep closing yourself off from everyone." He stared down at the huge piece of pseudo-gold. "Some things are more precious than gold or treasure. Don't think you can't have what Ezra gave you again. Life's too short to spend it all alone."

My lips curled back in a snarl that would make any Wolf shifter proud. "Don't lecture me about that, Kevin. Not now." I wrapped the blanket around myself in a few quick, jerky motions. "You should know I'm all bad luck. No good can come from being with me." I stalked to the other side of the dining room, keeping my back to him for a few minutes while I regained some composure. "Just look at the stupid rock."

Kevin's scowl returned in full swing. "Look. I'm doing the best I can for you. You feel like you're cursed. I get it. But you're not. If you were, I'd be able to sense it." He slouched into a kitchen chair and pulled his glasses from the top of his head to the bridge of his nose to get a better look at the golden ball. He didn't need them to see. They were magnifying glasses for the worn-out ancient texts he liked digging through.

Grudgingly, I took a few steps closer. I knew I was being a little harsh when he only wanted to help, but I wouldn't let him be next on my bad karma's hit list. That's why I'd gone to such lengths to separate myself from him, even if it hurt to turn my back on a friend who grieved just as deeply as I did. The fact that he'd told me to move on spoke greatly of his ability to put others before his own pain, but it didn't look like he was exactly following his own advice. However, having his support made me feel like at least someone else in this world cared if I lived or died, something I hadn't really felt worthy of in the past few months.

"Where did you find this?" He gaped as he pushed his glasses back onto his head. "I haven't really seen anything quite like it before." His voice wavered a little as he spoke, but I thought that might be residual emotion from our conversation. "Let me take it down to my lab and crack it open. I need to get a better look at it. If you don't mind, that is." He shifted abruptly back to his normal laid-back self.

Before I could answer, he headed for his laboratory. The wooden steps leading to it were worn from heavy use, with scorch marks and chemical burns marring the last four. The once light-colored walls had seen better days, and sported hasty white patches easily visible to the naked eye in one corner. The air carried the familiar scent of bleach and ammonia, which I'd grown used to in his lair. Kevin leaned over the central table, muttering under his breath about the rock's color details and making notes on a yellow legal pad.

"You definitely have something different here. See this pitting here on the surface?" He took off his glasses to hand to me, but I waved them away. "Gold plating would cover that." He strained a little when lifting it. "Hmm... Weight is off too. Where did you find this?" he asked, his voice holding echoes of awe. His gaze remained glued to the golden rock in his hand.

With the clearing weighed down by a heavy blanket of magic, I didn't give him too many details. The less he knew, the less chance there was of him getting hurt. I'd lost

enough friends and family already. "In the forest. I acciden-
tally dropped it a few times on my way here. Any idea what
it is?" I said, hoping he wouldn't ask for more specifics on
where I'd found it.

"None whatsoever. One thing I do know is it's not
natural, but it's not man-made, either. A few of my high-
level clients might have an idea of what it takes to do something like this. Don't hold your breath, though." Kevin set
the golden orb onto a copper plate close to his workbench.
With a few careful moves, he brought the copper plate
beneath his high-powered magnifying glass to get a better
look.

While he examined the surface of the rock, I shifted my
gaze to take in the basement. Various instruments and glass
vials neatly lined one desk. What looked like a cabinet filled
with chemicals took up an entire wall toward the back.
Some containers looked harmless, while others contained
eerie fluids that changed color every few seconds. A broken
glass beaker lay on one counter, with watery orange liquid
spreading across it. I kept my distance from that one. It
seemed that whatever I'd interrupted had taken all of his
attention. Tendrils of pent-up energy flowed from the liquid,
as if searching for a vessel. Thankfully it didn't have much
reach, or I'd be waiting upstairs. I made a mental note to
keep away from that area, and to be more patient when
knocking next time.

I turned my head to assess the rest of the room. Under
the fluorescent lights, the place had a relatively normal feel.
'Here lives Kevin the Nerd, not Kevin the Wizard,' it seemed
to say. The other workbench broke that illusion. It had a
ring of concentric circles drawn underneath it, which
glowed softly with a power of their own. No one could
mistake the contents of that section as anything you could

buy from a hardware store. Books and other paraphernalia sat on the corner desk. Next to it, the entire wall had an extended wood and steel bookshelf filled with various research books, some of which seemed oddly out of place, like a section on Japanese folklore next to his collection of Stephen King novels.

A cough drew my attention back to Kevin, and I made my way over to him as he completed his cursory examination.

"There's some serious magic around this thing," he said finally, and looked up at me. "I need more time with it to give you anything substantial. Can I keep it here for now?"

I nodded, having little use for the golden rock. None of my clients were likely to want it. Besides, I trusted Kevin not to 'misplace' it while investigating further. "No problem. Let me know when you find something. Be careful. One doesn't just find gold lying around like that."

Nodding, he led the way back upstairs. I followed close behind him, my raven eager to get back to the open air outside. When we reached the living room, I folded up the blanket as I watched him. "I mean it. I don't want to find out you did something stupid."

"Don't worry about me. I'll get back to you on what I learn about that aberrational beauty." Kevin took the blanket back, then frowned. "You know, he wouldn't want you to mourn him like this. He'd want you to move on. Get out of the house. Live a little."

I opened my mouth to rebut his statement, since I'd known Ezra better than him, but he closed the door in my face, leaving me standing on his doorstep with the cool night air tickling my bare flesh. Drawing in a shaky breath, I turned around and leaned my head back against the door. Trees lined his property to give some privacy, and I stared out into them as I brought myself back under control before the flight home.

The last thing I needed was to lose my concentration mid-flight and fall to my death.

Ugh... Why did I have to think that?

4

CODY

My coyote loved being out in the forest like this, but I knew he wanted to be running wild, not stalking these humans as they carefully hiked through the rough landscape. Getting out of the library had been a good idea, even if I might regret it tomorrow during my quizzes. Besides, if I sated the beast, he might be better behaved when we were done here.

Right. Who was I kidding?

So far, I hadn't sensed anything too unusual. The town had a plethora of shifters and wizards. Just recognizing that magic had recently taken place in a given area wasn't strange, the way the frat guy had suggested. This very well could be a bust, but I was already here. Might as well see this to completion before calling it a waste of my time.

While I might be willing to give up on my hunch, my grandmother had recently sensed some peculiar energy that disturbed her. She deserved to know what was going on if I did find something important.

"God, Donnie, how much farther? You said it would be just a quick stroll." The girl smacked Donnie's arm as he tried to wrap it around her waist. "If we don't come across this place soon, I'm going back. I will *so* not be killed in the woods by some crazy axe murderer because *you* wanted to get in my pants."

"Babe, don't get all mental. If I wanted to get in your pants that bad, we could've just done the deed in my dorm room. Seriously, my buddies wouldn't lie about this sort of thing. Rex knows if they did, I'd beat him up." He dropped his arms to his sides, but shot her an annoyed glare. "Just let me hold you, Mary. Your skin is freezing, since you stubbornly didn't bring a jacket. You did that on purpose, didn't you?"

Mary lifted her chin up in defiance. "Maybe." But she leaned into him as they walked, as if satisfied with Donnie's answer. She wrapped her arms over her stomach as he replaced his arm around her waist. "But you did say it wouldn't take that long to check this out."

"Yeah, sorry." He sighed, but the sound cut off with a rapid intake of air. "Holy shit!"

My ears perked up, and I darted forward to get a better look at whatever had startled Donnie. I froze in place when I saw it, and my eyes went wide. We'd definitely found the magical disturbance, and I knew without a doubt that it was from my family's artifact. A snarl formed in my throat, but I cut it off before it built into a full-fledged growl. The humans didn't need any more scares.

Ahead of me, the scene was one of beauty and destruction. Short, flowing strands of gold and silver hung on the branches of the few trees that still stood upright. Small rocks and boulders alike had been pulled from the earth and driven through the tree trunks. The torn ground made their paths easy to trace. Threads of pine needles and long grass sparkled along the trees like Christmas decorations.

No wildlife dared hang around to see the sight. The scent of magic overpowered the atmosphere, making my limbs feel like I was slogging through deep mud. To my nose, it smelled like tangy copper mixed with lavender. Strong tribal magic had been used here.

"Donnie... For once, I think we might have a chance." Mary spoke the words with awe. My coyote snarled again and bared his fangs, wanting them to show respect for the destruction that had happened here. The trickster part of me thought to spoil their romantic evening, but they weren't worth it. With a small huff, I pushed the thoughts aside and sniffed along the forest floor, hoping to find traces of who might've done this.

The cool, moist earth underneath my paws reinvigorated me as I put distance between myself and the disaster. How long had I walked in shoes on concrete and asphalt anyway? I let my coyote lead me for a moment, reveling in the joy of being out in the wild again. Here and there were signs of squirrels and other curious creatures, but their tracks grew more confused and fearful the closer they came to the new clearing. The strong scent of deer urine painted a picture of what it must've been like to witness the surprising destruction.

I circled around the bushes, letting the smells clear from my nose. The more I walked, the more evident it became how powerful the force behind the magic must have been. Older, rotting trees had fallen over outside of the initial blast radius, and small pebbles stripped the bark from trees as far as my eyes could see into the forest.

The humans had moved to one side of the new clearing for their rutting, and I was finally alone to check out the scene for myself.

Precious metals were spread along the trees and the

ground from the center of destruction outward. Strands of grass showed just how much power had been unleashed. A small fragment of gold had been torn into an extended string. The length of it was hot enough to burn a small batch of the grass underneath it. Silver threads pierced through an overhead branch, hanging limp like an odd strain of parasitic moss.

After tracking the scents in the area, I finally found magical ground zero, where the wizard had likely stood. The strong aroma of magic covered most of his identifying scents, but I caught a few details that might be useful. For one, he wore thick, insulated boots. The new smell of rubber made my coyote sneeze. The scent of unfiltered tobacco and wood spoke of a Native American pipe, like the one my grandmother smoked, but this one was newly crafted. As if someone had tried to placate the spirits of the talisman. But why the insulated boots?

The scene built a raw sense of fear in me. This looked like a patch of forest after a tornado. Whoever had used the talisman knew that he might be unable to control it, even by smoking the ceremonial pipe to appease the spirits. That unnerved me. Someone was playing around with a lot of magic, my people's power, without a care for whom or what would get hurt. But it did explain the isolated area. No witnesses, no property close by that might be damaged, and most importantly, he had time and privacy to prepare for the ceremony.

Anger flared inside me, and this time I let my snarl build into a growl. Deeper into the woods, a wolf wisely decided to take a detour around the new clearing. My coyote was as big as he was, but he probably knew from my scent that I wasn't what I seemed. The sound of the humans walking back to the clearing after their pleasure was finished set me off running. I dug my paws into the forest floor to pick up the speed.

Someone had found the talisman. My grandmother had been right. It wasn't destroyed. But it had fallen into hands of someone who knew enough to use it, yet lacked the wisdom not to.

My people knew that what you put out there always came back with a vengeance.

5

MORGANA

Afty last night's crazy discovery, I'd soaked in my garden tub for hours to relieve my sore muscles. But that didn't stop my raven from wanting to go for our typical early-evening flight over the forest. It was our version of exercise, more effective than jogging or push-ups.

We started our descent toward home as Nightmoon Creek came into view. I dove a little lower to the ground, but no one appeared to be nearby. I lightly touched down on my rooftop, taking a moment to shed my raven form. Sighing, I glanced between the creek and the forest with its colorful autumn leaves. The sight was absolutely breathtaking. If I hadn't been naked, I would've sat up there for hours.

I lived out in the sticks because I didn't like being too near other people. My instincts screamed at me to keep my distance and let no one close enough to hurt me when they eventually left—either because they found out just how messed up I was, or worse, because those around me had a bad habit of dying. I'd lost so many loved ones already, and I was barely twenty-one years old.

My childhood was littered with death and betrayal, and

I'd been bounced around from one foster home to another. Regardless of what Kevin said, at times I did feel cursed, as if my hardships weren't just bad luck. Was I the cause of all the pain? Being a shifter made me so different from everyone else that I didn't doubt it.

I hopped down from the roof and softly landed on my feet in the grass. The cool evening breeze sent shivers over my naked skin. I wasn't expecting any company, and the tree line on my property was designed with privacy in mind. No one could stumble upon my yard and see me like this, so I hadn't planned any clothes drops for quick dressing. The forecast had called for rain. Even though it hadn't come, I kept my clothes inside. A little water on my feathers or skin wouldn't hurt.

I rounded the corner of the house only to see a man knocking on my front door. I froze in place like a deer in headlights, blinking in surprise. How had I not noticed him when I was coming in to land? I'd scanned my surroundings, as I always did.

He turned toward me, and my legs kicked into high gear, propelling me back around the corner, out of sight. Modesty wasn't an issue, but I didn't flaunt my nudity when I had no idea who the person was or why they were here. It could be a human, or someone looking to hire me for a job. Granted, the latter was less likely, since I hadn't told anyone in town what I did, and none of my clients knew where I lived. This was supposed to be my sanctuary. The little piece of paradise I had in the world, aside from the sky.

"Sorry, miss. Didn't mean to come by unannounced, but I heard you could probably help me. Something of mine has been...lost. I need it found." He let out a sharp hiss of a sigh, but even though he came a little closer, he didn't turn the corner to face me.

I leaned against the building, closing my eyes for a brief moment. *Damn it.* This intrusion on my home turf bothered me. How had this man found me? I should probably listen to him and see what he wanted, although I really hated that he'd broken my place of refuge. But I'd have plenty of time to rage about that later. First, I needed to find something to cover up with if I was going to talk with him. Money wasn't good for me right now, and I aimed to be professional with potential clients. No matter what.

"Give me a moment, then I'll be able to talk with you further." I glanced around the corner at him, peeking out just my head and neck. He stood at average height, and his broad, muscular shoulders tapered into a narrow waist that made me think of a professional swimmer's physique. My mouth went dry as I wondered what his chest looked like.

He peeled off his jacket while I watched him. "You can borrow my coat." His biceps flexed as he held it out for me. I started to protest, but he tossed it on the grass and turned around. "I insist."

I leaned down and grabbed the leather jacket, keeping an eye on his back as I reached for it. For a guy as lean as he was, I thought the jacket might not cover me, but it did. It hung just to my upper thigh, showing lots of leg, but it could've been worse. I zipped it up and stepped around the corner.

He kept his gaze straight ahead, as if unsure whether to turn around. Although from the stiffening of his shoulders, I knew he could hear me approach. I still walked a little louder than I normally would.

The jacket rode up a little in the back, showing more skin than I wanted, and I tugged it down before I walked past to face him. "Hi."

The blond-haired man stared at me without speaking,

his blue gaze sliding down my body to my smooth legs. He fumbled out a few guttural sounds, then cleared his throat and tried again. "Uh, hi. Sorry. Guess I didn't expect..." He took a deep breath, letting it out slowly, then chuckled. "Yeah, I'm tongue-tied."

I wrapped my arms around me just under my chest. His reaction made me a little nervous. It had been a while since any guy had looked at me like that, and I wasn't sure I liked it—not after losing the one man who'd managed to get close to me. Grief clawed at my throat, forcing up all the feelings I tried so hard to shut down.

"That's fine, Mr...?" I trailed off expectantly.

"Call me Cody. No need to be formal with me." The guy grinned, shoving his hands in his pockets. There weren't any goosebumps on his bare arms, so he wasn't actually cold. His gaze rose toward the twilight sky, where the moon slowly waxed toward full. Could he be a shifter too? If he was, he certainly didn't appear very intimidating. I couldn't get a good read on him, aside from his obvious attraction to my human form.

"Okay then, Cody. How can I help you?" I brought my gaze up to meet his. He had a sort of frat boy appeal to him, and I wondered if he was attending Hastings-Albrecht University. I'd given up my dreams of college as a preteen. Instead of school, I went with what I was best at—finding treasure like my dad. That was learned outside of the classroom.

"Well..." He looked around the woods surrounding my house, as if something would jump out at him. "Can we go inside? I don't feel comfortable discussing—" He stopped himself, then flashed me a friendly smile. "Errr...yeah. Besides, I'm sure you'd feel a lot better in there too." He lowered his gaze again before dragging it back to my eyes.

I nodded. I'd definitely feel more comfortable with him not staring at me like that. I cleared my throat, but instead of saying anything, I turned on my heel and walked toward the front door.

"Turn around please," I said. I'd have to bend over and potentially show my butt because I kept my spare key under one of the potted plants. Carrying keys in my raven form was difficult at best.

He frowned at me, but did as I asked. "So, uh, how long have you been in town?"

I glanced up at his back, wishing he'd stop trying to make small talk. But he was trying to be civil, I guess, and we were both in a kind of awkward position. He probably hadn't expected the person he needed help from to be strolling around naked.

"Let's just get inside and discuss what brings you here, okay?" I didn't want to be rude to Cody, but I desperately wanted to get this over with, especially after my conversation with Kevin. Even if I knew it was probably a good idea, how could he think I'd be able to move on so quickly? Pain surrounded me, and I could barely recognize myself at times.

When I slid the key into the lock, Cody turned around. He frowned at me, his face a little more serious than it'd been before. I couldn't say I blamed him. I'd been a little more firm than I'd intended, but a long, hot bath was calling to me. The flight home had made my aches and pains turn into sharp, shooting stabs going through my arms and back.

I rolled my shoulders and neck a little, before I realized what that might do to the jacket, and promptly stopped. He wasn't casting admiring stares anymore, and I didn't know how to feel about that. Maybe I'd enjoyed his gaze on me. Maybe I did need to stop getting in my own way. One thing was for sure: if he was here for a job of any kind, then he was off-limits for the duration. I wasn't the kind of gal to mix business with pleasure.

We walked into the living room, and I waved my hand toward the couch for him, while I claimed the armchair. It was best to keep a little bit of space between us. I wasn't exactly sure how much he could see when I sat in his jacket. I should've just gone off to my bedroom to change, but the sooner he left, the sooner I'd regain my space.

I grabbed a notepad and a pen from the end table, which I kept there for business calls. I always like to be prepared when I need to remember information. My memory's pretty solid, but I've gotten things mixed up before, and I don't ever want to repeat that experience.

"So, Cody, tell me why you're here." I held the pen over the paper and looked up at him expectantly.

His frown had deepened, and he looked from me to his hands. "To the point, I guess. You probably get a lot of people needing your help, but this is different. I'm not trying to get rich or find some kind of archaic curiosity." He let out a breath then took in another. "You know the tornadoes that ripped through in April, right?"

I nodded, not sure where he was going with this.

"My family lost the house we've lived in for many generations." He shook his head and ran his hands through his blond hair, keeping his head bowed like that for a moment. "We had many irreplaceable Native American artifacts, one of which had magical properties." He raised his gaze to mine when he said it, as if expecting scorn or disapproval.

I gave neither, since I knew magic existed. He didn't need to try to convince me about that. I'd dealt with the consequences of someone playing with it before. "Go on."

He dropped his gaze to the pink, white, and grey Southwestern-style rug on the floor beneath the coffee table for a moment. "When the house was destroyed, we dug through the wreckage, and we were able to find most of our belongings, except my family's sacred talisman. We looked for it everywhere, and when we didn't find it, we assumed it hadn't survived." Letting out a long sigh, he frowned up at me. "It seems like we were wrong."

My heart clenched in my chest, and warning bells rang out in my head. No... No way could I take this on. Not when I'd lost Ezra in my last search for a magical artifact. This wasn't a good fit for me anymore. If he needed to find some buried treasure, or wanted me to search through some catacombs in Italy, I was his girl.

This? No, I didn't want to rip that scab off.

6

CODY

Something akin to panic flashed through the lady treasure hunter's eyes at the mention of the talisman. I'd heard from my archeology professor who used her services that she handled things like this, so I wasn't sure why she looked so worried. Maybe she knew more than I did. Regardless, the whole encounter had started off on the wrong foot.

"It's out there," I continued. "I saw proof of it last night in the forest."

"Proof?" She cocked her head at me like a bird, all while scribbling in her notepad. My coyote leaned forward, not keen on having to explain ourselves.

"Yeah, I—" Her cell phone rang, cutting me off, and I sat back on the couch, trying to remain patient. My coyote saw the woods outside and paced in my chest, ready to run free again. The red duffel bag I used to carry clothes was tucked behind a tree out of sight. We'd cut through the forest to come here, but it was never enough for him. College had made us more restless than usual. Or maybe it was the magic. Power hummed quietly beneath my feet, spreading out from the ley-line, and the coyote reacted each time it waxed and waned. I pondered that while she took the call, doing my best not to listen in.

"Morgana, I'm glad you picked up. There's something you should—" Apparently, my curious coyote didn't mind snooping, not that I was surprised by that after the library fiasco. But his inquisitive nature had been helpful finding out about the talisman, so I couldn't be too hard on him. After all, it was in his nature to snoop and be aware of his surroundings. On the other hand, she deserved her privacy, but how could I explain moving away so as not to hear both ends of the phone call? Sooner or later, I would slip if I paid too close attention, but that didn't seem to worry my coyote.

She returned her gaze to me and pursed her lips as if in thought. "Sorry, Kevin, now isn't a good time. I'll call you back later." When she hung up, she messed with the phone a little more as if sending a text, then set it aside again. There was an elegance to her movements that drew me in. I was impressed that she'd set aside time to talk with me, someone she didn't know, after I showed up unannounced. Sure, she was beautiful, but there was more to it than that.

She seemed to be around my age, but I'd never seen her around Woodland Creek. With a little over three thousand residents, that wasn't easy. The college was a decent size, but not big enough that I wouldn't have seen her before, so I could only wonder if she locked herself away from everyone else on purpose. I preferred to have some distance from the everyday worries of humans myself. It was hard enough trying to survive the college lifestyle with a rambunctious coyote. Bars and other normal hangouts weren't my thing.

I couldn't help but drink in the brisk, somewhat aggressive, black-haired woman in front of me. This chick was different. I could tell she was a shifter, since she didn't smell like any human I'd ever been around. The way she carried herself and her focused attention spoke of strong self-control brought to mind something predatory. Regardless of the type of shifter she was, she exuded strength in a no-nonsense way that was admirable, even though I sensed an enormous amount of pain floating off her. She came across a bit like a wounded animal, and I hated seeing anyone like that.

"We should grab some coffee tomorrow." The words spilled from my lips before I could hold them back. At her frown, I continued in a rush, "So I can tell you more about the talisman and the proof, of course. Besides, it's getting late, and you have to call Kevin back." I hated how desperate I sounded, when I'd never struggled to ask anyone out before. The slightest bit of jealousy crept into my voice, and I gave her a crooked smile to defuse it. I felt like an idiot, but my coyote seemed to approve.

She frowned at me, watching me closely for a moment as if I might pounce, but then nodded in acceptance. "Okay, that sounds fine." Picking her phone back up, she tapped it a few times, then glanced at me once more. "How about four o'clock?"

Penciled in. Ouch. My teeth ground at her needing to schedule time with me, but I forced myself to relax my jaw. The last thing I wanted was for her to see how much it annoyed me. It wasn't exactly a new experience. My siblings never wanted to spend any time with their white brother. They allocated me as little time as possible, and instead played with others who shared their heritage more strongly.

She was probably just busy with other clients and didn't want to overlap appointments. "Yeah, that's good. My classes end around three, so I'll be free." Something about her made me want to try for more than a strictly business relationship.

Maybe I was a sucker for rejection. Who knew? Maybe it was my coyote hoping for the best, a place to finally belong. Someone to spend time with who mattered to me.

With even my own blood not wanting to be near me, I'd had more than my share of trouble growing up. Part of me always longed to head out into the woods and lose myself. If I followed my coyote, maybe he would be my light in the dark. But I never gave in, fearing the isolation from humans might twist me into a feral inhuman monster, like the witikos of Cree folklore.

"Good. If you have any pictures of the item or the proof, please bring them with you tomorrow. I..." Pausing, she fidgeted with the phone for a moment, scratching at its edge as if nervous. "This doesn't mean we have a deal, you understand. I just want to get all the facts before I decide whether I'll be taking on the job. It's better for me to have a full understanding of what I might be looking for. Small details make all the difference." She stood in my jacket, and I glanced down at her long legs again before I could stop myself. Her gaze followed mine, and she drew her arms around her chest. "Just stay here for a moment. I'll be right back with your jacket."

I watched her go, unable to help myself. Beneath my skin, my coyote nipped at me, wanting me to follow and give her a great time to wash away that sadness weighing her down. Then I'd be no better than that creep Donnie...but he ultimately hadn't been rejected. I ran my hands through my hair again. If she didn't take me on, what would I do? I hadn't really thought that might be a possibility, even though I was a college student living paycheck-to-paycheck, and I bet she catered to the wealthy. Her house was much bigger than my family's had been before the tornado.

She had to agree to help me.

7

MORGANA

I shut the bedroom door behind me, feeling my pulse start to race. My breath came out in harsh pants, as if I'd just run a freaking marathon. The way I'd felt in front of Cody was too much for me. I didn't want to feel any different about him than I did any other client, but something about him had caught me off-guard. He was charming and nice to me. Something about him made me think of how Ezra had been at the beginning of our relationship. I slammed that mental door shut and bit my lower lip, hard.

I'd shrugged out of a pair of jeans and red t-shirt earlier before I'd gone flying, so I slipped into a pair of red lacy panties and a matching bra before putting that outfit back on. They had only been worn for a few hours, so the jeans and shirt weren't nasty. Besides, I'd been pretty clean after that long bath last night. Memories of it made me crave another. Cody would need the coat if he were to walk wherever home was for him. The weather was beginning to feel more and more wintry. I looked down at the brown leather jacket and brought it to my nose, inhaling his scent before I caught what I'd done.

Get a hold of yourself, girl! I was going birdbrained after talking with Kevin last night, and then being around Cody. That needed to stop. I was a strong, independent female. Ezra had been the love of my life. That was over. It didn't matter what Kevin said. No one else needed to be put at risk for the sake of my relationship status.

However, I did need this job. Kevin had one point. I did need to get out of the house more. Keeping myself locked up and torturing myself over my inability to save Ezra wasn't helping me. That behavior did more harm than good.

I opened the door to my bedroom and walked back out into the living room to the sight of Cody's strong back as he stared out of the sliding glass doors. The snug shirt he wore gave an excellent view of the delicious expanse of muscles underneath.

"Here's your jacket," I said, laying it on the couch where he'd been sitting. "I'll think about whether or not I'll take your job. Like I mentioned, bring whatever information you have tomorrow. I'd like to know what I might be searching for." The last time someone had held back info, the person I'd love had died...and that part definitely was my fault, whether I wanted it to be true or not.

But I couldn't keep beating myself up over past failures. I'd learned a very hard lesson, and someone I'd loved had paid the price. Now I was hopefully smarter, and maybe I'd be more aloof about relationships in the future, especially when they intersected my career. For better or worse, I was a treasure hunter. This was my living, and I needed to stop hiding from it.

"Thanks." He turned to face me, and took a few steps to cross the space between the window and where I stood by the couch. "I didn't catch your name before...?" He held out his hand to me, and I looked at it a moment before accepting his.

"My name is Morgana. Since you found out about me, I would've thought that you might know that already." Shrugging a shoulder, I grabbed my notepad from the end table and flipped to a blank page to jot down my number.

"Yeah, I guess you're right." He gave me a roguish grin, and I caught myself melting a little. "Someone told me about you through e-mail. They didn't know who you were, just that there was someone who finds things that lived in these cabins by the creek."

"Good to know." I raised both of my eyebrows, surprised that I'd managed to get a reputation among people in town. Who was talking about me? Who would come looking for me once they knew my talents? The idea concerned me. If Cody had found out about me, then other, less savory types might as well.

He nodded. "It's all good. No worries."

Still, my feeling of unease didn't go away. "Well, I'll see you tomorrow at four o'clock. How about Woodland Creek Coffee?" I forced a smile.

Cody grabbed his jacket from the couch and nodded. "Yeah, sounds great. I'll be there." The atmosphere of the room shifted, as if he could sense my discomfort. He turned away from me, and I followed him to the door.

After seeing him off, I decided to call Kevin back. He probably wouldn't be going to bed anytime soon. He always claimed he did his best work in the wee hours of the morning. But it was better that I see what he wanted sooner, rather than later. He'd sounded too relieved when I'd picked up. That meant something.

The phone rang and rang and rang. Of course, he wasn't answering. I sighed. It figured. He was probably back in his basement with his earbuds in again. It was any wonder he could still hear with how loud he played them.

I dropped onto the couch and brought my knees up to my chest. Cody's smile had dazzled me in a way no other guy had since Ezra. He'd been the one for me. For me to have any shred of emotions kind of scared me, but maybe it was good to feel again. I didn't want to be the hollow shell of a woman that I'd been when I'd come home from South America.

8

MORGANA

I arrived a little early for my meeting with Cody. I'd wanted to gather my thoughts before seeing him again. Last night, I hadn't been fully on my game. The conversation with Kevin and the hard flight had both thrown me off. I needed to brush it all off and think about the work. I'd gone into isolation before to keep myself from getting hurt again, but now I thought that if I could throw myself back into my work, I might start healing.

Granted, this might not be the best return to treasure hunting, but at least it was something. My usual contacts had dried up a little after I'd fallen off the grid. If I showed them I was back, I could get my spot back. And if I wanted to pay my bills, I needed this job.

Woodland Creek Coffee was located in Old Town. Its atmosphere was cozy and quaint. Kind of like the town itself, which was charming in its own way, with everything one could possibly need. That was one of the reasons I enjoyed living here, even if I didn't roam around town often. People sipped their coffees as they read their books, used their computers, or just gossiped. Two people glanced up as I entered, but most kept their attention elsewhere.

I wasn't really one for coffee, so I ordered a hot chocolate before claiming a quiet spot in a corner away from the other patrons. When Cody got here, I wanted some semblance of privacy, even though I knew the town had other shifters. Old Town was the go-to locale for magical beings. The only way we'd get true privacy would be to go back to my house, but last night had been so awkward. I didn't trust myself to have him back there.

The steamy dreams I'd had of him made heat warm my face despite the cool weather outside. Cody seemed like a nice guy. I didn't want him to get tangled up with me.

My phone buzzed, and I looked down at it to see I'd gotten a new e-mail from another potential client. When it rained it poured, it seemed. My thumb hovered over the e-mail icon, but just then the door chimed to signal a new arrival. Cody. I quickly slid the phone into my purse, knowing I'd be able to check it later.

He sauntered over to the table first, sliding that mass of well-defined muscle into the chair before me. I bit my lower lip, hating the shift in my thoughts. Like he was some hunky piece of...man. I shook my head.

"Hey, Morgana. I hope you weren't waiting too long. I got a later start than I'd planned. I dropped off my books at my dorm room before heading over, and my roommate felt like talking."

"No problem." I hadn't realized he had that far of a walk, or I would've met him closer to his campus. Not that there seemed to be much over there, but I guess it didn't matter now. "Are you going to order something before we get started?" I nodded to the counter where a young barista watched us, or more likely him, while we talked. I looked away from her, because if I didn't, I might march over there and get in her face. Couldn't she see that we were together here? Of course, not as a couple. No. Just business.

"Yeah, if you don't mind, I think I will." He headed over to the counter, and I watched him go, grimacing at the fact that my eyes raked over him the way his had done to me last night, resting on his perfectly molded backside. He glanced over his shoulder at me, and I caught his grin. How had he known I'd been staring? I turned back to the table, fixing my gaze on my cooled hot chocolate as heat burned my cheeks. How freaking embarrassing...

I reached into my purse for my phone to check the e-mail, when he came back to the table with a coffee and two pastries. He set one in front of me, and I looked up in surprise. I was never one to turn away a pastry, though.

He took a sip of his coffee before reaching for the back-pack at his side. "This is what I could find on the artifact. We didn't have any pictures of it directly, but there are a couple sketches from some book on Native American shamanism." He sighed. "Sorry I couldn't come up with anything more precise. But I went back to the forest and took a couple of pictures of the damage with my phone." He slid an orange folder toward me, and I peeked inside to see some photo-copies from a book and a few printed pictures of what looked like the aftermath of a bomb going off in a clear-ing...or a tornado, except with glitter and Christmas tinsel? That startled me a little. From the large collection of boul-ders, it seemed to be near the area where I'd found the golden ball the other night.

He wasn't my usual clientele, but I could tell this talisman meant a lot to him. However, I had bills. Would he be able to pay me for my time? I hoped we'd be able to work something out. I couldn't disregard his problem on the basis of payment alone, especially seeing the devastation done to that section of the forest. If whoever wielded the artifact used it in the town, people could get hurt, and I wouldn't have that on my conscience. Besides, his parents could have money... It was a family artifact after all. But he'd said they were rebuilding after the tornado. I wasn't heartless.

Cody sat back in his chair, watching me as if he searched for something in my face. I guess I didn't blame him since I'd been pretty reluctant to work for him last night. I still wasn't sure that this was something I wanted to get into, but it was the right thing to do. As long as I didn't have anyone else around who might get hurt, I would make sure to protect those in need from what might happen if the talisman was activated again. It didn't matter what happened to me. I'd survived unfortunate situations before.

"So, what do you think?" he asked when I'd let the silence between us carry on longer than I probably should have. "Will you take me on?"

I opened my mouth, then closed it, searching for words. "Yes, I'll do it." After I took another sip of my hot chocolate, I slid him a form I gave all my clients. "Sign and e-mail this to me at your convenience. Once that's done, I'll get to work."

He jerked upward in his chair as if shocked by my answer. Before I knew what he was doing, he pulled a pen from his pocket and skimmed the page quickly, before signing it right there. I grimaced at his eagerness, but maybe I'd be the same way in his position. When he slid it back my way, I folded it in thirds before putting it in my purse. "Great. I'll get started today." I lowered my voice to make sure no one around could easily overhear, and tapped the folder. "Do you have the coordinates of where this happened?"

He frowned and shook his head. "No. I didn't think to look them up, but I could take you by there if you want."

The thought of spending more time with him was appealing, especially in a place where we wouldn't be under the watchful eye of the barista, but I shook away his offer. If whoever had done that sort of magic was still around, I didn't want him to be in any more danger than necessary. "No, that's okay. I'm sure I'll find it."

"You're sure?" He raised an eyebrow at me as if I was crazy.

I was kind of used to that.

As a Raven shifter, I could cover a helluva lot more ground than any person on two legs. My position in the sky granted me a broad panorama of the forest in great detail with my raven's eyesight. We were used to going on less information than what he'd provided. Besides, I'd been near that area during my previous flight, so I knew approximately where to go.

He shifted in his chair as if anxious. His eyes darted around the room, and I spotted a wizard from one of the founding families. I could never remember their names, probably because I wasn't sure I wanted to get mixed up with them. Magic and mayhem weren't high on my list of things to mess with, given my history.

"Are you okay?" I asked, placing my hand over his before I realized what I was doing.

He froze and looked at me in the eye. Something was different there, a little more primal than it had been. I cocked my head to the side, my raven flapping her wings in frustration. "Sorry." I started to pull away, but he held onto my hand.

"I'm okay. I just get a little antsy when I'm indoors for too long." He smiled, but it was a toothy grin that spoke of some

43

fanged animal rather than the cool, calm guy I'd met last night.

For a moment, I considered pulling away a little more strongly, but I knew he wasn't trying to intimidate me. Perhaps he wasn't human. I couldn't decide if I thought he was something more. I was intrigued, but it wasn't my place to ask, especially not here in front of all these people. While the supernatural was an open secret around town, I didn't know if he was open with that side of him or not.

"Mind if we get out of here and take a walk?" he asked. "I could use some fresh air."

Glancing back toward the counter at the nosy barista, I nodded, taking my paper cup of half-drunk hot chocolate with me. I could use some air too. Too bad people didn't look kindly upon women stripping naked and turning into ravens in the middle of town, or I wouldn't have need for a car. My natural form was a much more efficient method of travel. Although, there was something about those powerful machines. I looked to my black Dodge Charger, parked in front of the coffee shop, and smiled. Just because I preferred flying didn't mean I couldn't enjoy earthly luxuries.

We walked along the sidewalk on Old High Street, past a tattoo shop, the real estate office, and a bookshop. A companionable silence stretched between us. We cut across the road and behind the Pond & Duck Restaurant to a walking path that circled the lake. He didn't say much as we watched the ducks quack at us, but neither did I.

"So," I said, finally breaking the silence between us midway around the lake. "Anything else you can think of regarding this talisman?" I glanced to my right at him. My gaze zeroed in on the way his shirt clung to his muscles. I couldn't fight my growing attraction for him, even if it was the last thing I wanted.

Focus on the job, not on him.

He shrugged. "No. Just be careful." Something in the way he said that made me pause. Perhaps he cared about what might happen to me... Or I could be hunting for something scarier than I realized.

9

CODY

After seeing Morgana stare at the barista more than a few times, I knew she was growing as uncomfortable in the coffee shop as I was. The wizard and other magical beings in there set me on edge when we were discussing such a sensitive subject. Besides, my coyote couldn't stop drooling over how beautiful Morgana looked today in her tight black empire waist top and blue jeans that hugged her every curve. It was all I could do to keep my mind on the subject. I should've been concentrating on getting back the talisman, but I really just wanted to know if she had a boyfriend.

I didn't like seeing the hesitation in her eyes as I asked her to take care, as if she wasn't used to hearing those words. What kind of an existence did she lead? I kept thinking back to the 'Kevin' she'd been on the phone with yesterday. The thought of him being her boyfriend frustrated me, even though it shouldn't.

I let her lead after a while walking around the lake. Silence descended once again as we looped back around toward the coffee shop. She tossed her paper cup in a recycle bin in front of the bank. We walked across Old High Street and stopped in front of a black sports car. I raised an eyebrow at her, a bit surprised by her mode of transportation. Morgana was a surprising kind of gal, and I wanted to know more of her secrets. She seemed like she might have a lot of good ones.

Before I could stop myself, I asked, "Are you in a relationship with someone?" It was pretty damn brazen. While I might've been a confident guy, I wasn't normally like this.

She looked up at me with something akin to shock on her face. "Excuse me?"

I opened my mouth to apologize, but she spoke first. "That's not any of your business. I'm working a job for you, against my own better judgment. I don't know what you've heard about me, but I do not have relationships with my clients." She stomped toward her car door, but I got there first, blocking her from opening it. "Get out of my way, Cody."

"Wait, please. I'm sorry, okay?" I grimaced as she pushed against my chest, but I didn't budge. I couldn't lose her help because of my own stupidity. "It was silly of me to ask..." A few women walked past, giving us uneasy looks and making me feel even more like a jerk than I already did. "But it wasn't your reputation that made me ask. I..." I squeezed my hands into fists, trying to get the words out of my mouth, even though I'd had no problem with that a few moments ago. "I admire you, okay? I like you. I'm sorry I asked like that, but I'm not sorry because I would like to hang out with you."

She frowned up at me, not looking quite as hostile anymore. Just...confused. "I don't think that's a good idea."

It was my turn to frown. What? How could she say that it wasn't a good idea? I didn't care if she didn't have relationships with clients. I wouldn't be her client forever. My coyote growled, and the sound trickled from my lips. I coughed, trying to distract her attention from the sound, but I knew by the questioning look on her face that she'd caught it.

Morgana widened her eyes at me, but something about her posture changed a little. "I'll drive you back to campus. Get in."

I raised both eyebrows at her, but did as she said.

She started the car and threw it into reverse, zipping out of the spot while another car tried to ram past, forcing them to stop. "First of all, no, I'm not in a relationship." The car behind us honked their horn a few times, and she muttered a few curses under her breath. When we were off and away from them, she glanced at me and shook her head. "You probably see me as some strong chick with a pretty face, but even if I liked you too, I don't think getting anywhere near me would be a good idea." She let out a shaky sigh. "I'm not good with holding onto people."

"What's that supposed to mean?" It wasn't my business, but if she was going to give that kind of reason, I wanted to know.

"Every time I get close to someone, they end up going away." Her hands shook, and she clenched them tighter on the steering wheel. "Instead of causing any more trouble for anyone, it's just best for me not to go there again." But when she looked my way, I wondered for a moment if that was as hard for her to say it as it was for me to hear it.

I didn't feel quite as pissed off anymore. I could understand where she was coming from. Losing a lot of people close to them would make anyone unwilling to connect with others. I sometimes wondered if my own desire to connect wasn't because I'd never really known that kind of love. I'd never really had anyone worthwhile.

I looked up as we approached campus and glanced over at her as she slowed. "I'm truly sorry for your loss, but don't think I'll let this go so easily. You deserve to be happy again." I gave her a half-smile, not feeling like I could give a whole one. "Let me know when you find out news on the talisman." Her eyes watered a little, and I climbed out of the car, unable to watch her cry.

It was time for me to visit my grandmother and tell her what was going on. If anyone could give me more information on the talisman, it was her. I was concerned about Morgana going after it alone. I'd seen the damage it could cause. While I didn't want to insert myself into her life, I was serious when I said she deserved more from life. She deserved happiness.

I pushed my bag up higher on my shoulder and headed to my dorm room. It'd be easier for me to travel to my grandmother's if I was in coyote form. I was faster on four legs, and after that incident with Morgana, he was ready to run off the stress we were both feeling.

10

CODY

The thick set of oaks that lined the well-trodden path to my grandmother's house were ancient. When the Miami tribe first settled in the area, it was said that the spirit of nature herself gave a powerful shaman the trees. Now, many generations later, the trees still grew, even in adversity and dry seasons. Some thought it was a blessing, or magic at work, but I knew that my grandmother went to great lengths to care for the trees each day. It was her way to keep in touch with the legacy given to her for safekeeping.

My paws sank a little into the fertile ground as I made my way toward her home. In my mouth, I carried a red duffel bag with a change of clothes. It bounced with each step, but I paid it little attention. The air was silent to human ears, but for mine it was alive with the whispers of unspoken secrets. Tribal magic hung heavily in the air, permeating the forest all around me. It charged the edges of my fur, revitalizing me with its presence.

Despite the run, my coyote and I were eager to feel the wind rush along our fur as we darted through the forest. It seemed to be the only time my mind was clear anymore, not clouded by unnecessary garbage that had little to do with everyday life. I could go for weeks without running through the forest, but lately it had become a constant itch beneath my skin, the fur within desperate to find a path of least resistance to push through.

Before I'd made it halfway to the house, the door opened. My grandmother walked onto the porch, her wizened frame old and frail. Her features were always unreadable, but the light of clarity in her eyes remained. "I was told you were on your way, Grandson. Come up here. The forest is uneasy," she said, waving me closer. Her voice carried easily across the distance between us.

Picking up my pace, I dragged the bag of clothes up to her porch. Without asking for permission, I let the shift take hold of me. She'd lived with shamans and shifters all the years I had known her. Her eyes were turned toward the road while my spine twisted back into its human configuration and my fur made way to my pale skin.

When I first learned to shift, she'd been there to guide me. She had been there for everyone in the tribe, whenever they had a problem that needed her attention. No one ever called her. She simply knew when to be there.

My shift was over almost as soon as it had begun. I smirked as I caught an appraising look from her.

"Down to a less than a minute. Good." She nodded, pride evident in her voice.

I opened the small duffel bag and pulled on my clothes while speaking to her. "Yes, the coyote is ready to roam Running Deer. It's a welcome change from the paved world of humans. Could we step inside? I need to talk to you," I asked cautiously. One didn't boss around a shaman, regardless of how close one was to them. That's one of the things my grandmother had managed to drill into my thick skull—respect your family.

She opened the door for me, then followed me inside. The open layout of her house was a reminder of the older days of living in the plains, yet the solid wooden walls provided nice additional shelter for winter. The walls had a variety of tools and hunting equipment lining one side, with a massive bearskin rug taking up the middle of the floor, in front of the fireplace. The smell of watery soup, tobacco, and burnt pine mixed with more typical household smells.

Without waiting for her instruction, I walked over to a picture of our family taken years ago. At the center, my father was holding my mother in a tender embrace, while the children sat in front of them. In the background, my grandmother stood, watchful as ever over the couple.

While I was looking at the photo, my grandmother went to the small stove in the corner and poured us both a steaming mug of tea. Apparently, the spirits had been very specific about when I would arrive.

"What is so urgent that the grandson I raised would visit me?" she asked, her voice calm as usual. She handed me one of the cups and sat down in a chair before the fireplace.

"Sorry to interrupt your evening, but I need to talk with you. All this time you've said that the artifacts we lost weren't destroyed. Well, I believe you're right. I think someone has found one of them," I began tentatively. With a nod from her, I shared what I'd found in the forest. By the time I'd finished telling her about the destruction, the tea in my hands had cooled enough to be drinkable.

"Someone has found it. There's little question about that now. Do you know what it is, Cody? It's the talisman of an old wizard that lived among our people. With no respect for nature, he tricked the spirits into aiding him. When the white man came the first time, he saw their lust for gold and land. He spoke about riches and wealth...doom and curses. The spirits listened, imbuing that into the talisman. Whoever has the talisman must tread lightly, lest they anger the spirits within," she said with a sigh, pouring herself more tea.

"A wizard did that?" Knowing she didn't often open up about the older times, I hoped she would be kind enough to share more details.

"Yes. Listen with those coyote ears when I speak." She cast me a stern frown. "The wizard paid no respect to the living world around him. Shamans guide and protect their people and their surroundings. They act as a bridge between our world and the spirits. Wizards live by their own rules. Not all know, respect, or protect what they possess. Those that lead selfish or irresponsible lives will always face the consequences.

"This wizard spoke to the ground and to the air about his wants. Many spirits answered his pleas, and they need to be satisfied," she said, staring into the fire. Her eyes were focused on something only she could see. "What concerns me, Grandson, is that whoever uses the artifact does not know its full power. They play around with it like a toy, not understanding where or how it got its magic. Smoking a pipe and paying respects is something anyone can learn how to do. Knowing how, and why or why not to use the power, is a far greater lesson. It's like with your kind. One must respect and be one with themselves. If a shifter is out of balance, they are restless, wandering away from what they call home and seeking out things they don't need." Her knowing eyes now locked on mine. Power, and an iron will, lay behind her stare.

She nodded in satisfaction, as if she'd taught me enough.

But I couldn't help but feel the sting of her remark. My coyote didn't like it either, and locking her gaze to mine had been a show of dominance. "It's hard enough when my own family doesn't want to spend time with me. Even my cousin, Jacy, no longer responds to my calls. I know I look different from them, but am I not part of the same family?" I said quietly to her, my voice heavy with emotion.

Shaking her head, she frowned at me with sadness and understanding in her eyes. "They don't know how to behave. You are Coyote to them. Trickster and playful, but you are also the white man. They aren't used to that. Coyotes are usually found in pureblooded family lines. Somehow, you move beyond that. Jacy has been distant lately, and out hunting for a while. The spirits have spoken of him going through a season of trials, working out his own path in life. He is an adult, and we need to respect that. He will return to the family, or find his own way through life." Grandmother sighed and waved her hand at me. "Most importantly, if you find whoever has the talisman, it needs to be returned at once. No one will be safe until it is home. From what you described, the user has little to no control of it, beyond waking up the spirits. Trouble is brewing, and containing it is our responsibility. I'll reach out to others so they can keep their eyes and ears open. Maybe the spirits will be with us and someone has seen something." She smiled toothily.

"I hope so," I said, climbing to my feet. "I should let you get some rest." At her nod, I headed for the door.

Outside, the evening had turned into nighttime. My coyote stirred, eager for a quick run home. With a smile on my lips, I stretched and let the change overtake me again. I'd be dead tired in the morning, but none of that mattered now.

11

MORGANA

I sat down and let my mind wander a moment. Coffee with Cody had been nice, but I couldn't help but feel so vulnerable sometimes with him. Why on earth did I mention Ezra to him? Something about him made me feel like I could trust him. Even my raven didn't mind his presence. Typical humans made her agitated and a little uneasy, since she was a solitary beast. I walked over to my computer, wanting to verify some details about his story. Never trust a client, no matter how detailed they are about the object needing to be retrieved.

Sitting down in my chair, I waited for the computer to wake up from its electronic slumber. Some days were spent more in front of the computer than out in the field, much to my raven's chagrin. She'd rather have me fly across the landscape, looking for any and every minor detail for hours, rather than spend fifteen minutes on Google. Search engines made life a lot easier. A few quick and snappy queries and, voila, an instant library of detail about some object's history or legend. Digging through shelves in the actual library to read books was mostly a thing of the past. Thank God for technology.

My raven felt like bouncing up and down, ready to attack something out of sheer boredom, as I searched for truth in an electric sea of knowledge. Ten excruciating minutes later—for the raven at least—I found what I'd needed. Cody had been truthful.

A stray tornado had hit the area in April, destroying several houses. The weathermen who had reported on it stated that it was a highly unusual one, appearing out of thin air. One moment the weather radar had been normal, the next an insignificant thunderstorm in the area had turned into a tornado. There had been minimal rotation, and almost no warning signs for people in its path. Of course, a scientist had come up to the media only two days later, stating that a change in the upper atmosphere earlier that day had resulted in a sudden and massive pressure change, allowing the tornado to form. The media had gobbled up the story, and no one had decided to check the facts behind it.

Residents had begun reconstruction slowly. The tornado had also torn through a small section of the forest. Another article had mentioned the local chief of police requesting that hikers in the area be cautious, as the tornado might have disturbed local wildlife, and to keep an eye out for any missing historic relics, promising there would be a small reward given for the effort.

I was about to look further into Cody's personal details, to ensure that he was from the nearby tribe, even though his coloring seemed more Nordic than Native American, when an e-mail message dropped into my inbox. It was marked 'urgent,' with receipt request on being opened. It was linked to the one I'd received just before Cody and I had sat down for coffee. This James McGuire seemed in a hurry to have his message read. My interest was piqued, and I opened the email.

Mr. McGuire was very interested in getting immediate assistance with obtaining an item of 'obvious value,' and he'd been made aware that I had found something relating to it. He would cover all the usual expenses, and make sure I was compensated for the urgency. There was even a promise of assistance and protection, should I need it while I would be working for him. And he *requested* I reach out to him immediately in order to get my first paycheck. The retainer amount specified was higher than my usual one for local jobs. Was this for something overseas? I didn't have time for that right now. Besides, something felt off about this.

I was accustomed to customers who required immediate assistance, but even among those who were overly bossy and thought they could order everyone around at their own whim, the email still stood out like a sore thumb. I normally worked through a known set of intermediate contacts, but this e-mail had been sent to me directly. Asking for receipts on opening was normal, but customers normally wanted a degree of discretion about themselves, or worked through their lawyers. Either this man had influence, or the matter was urgent enough to him that he didn't even try to hide who he was.

This had also come up shortly after things went haywire in Running Deer, and after meeting Cody. Could this be an offer for another item of value in this area? But the price... It didn't add up. Artifacts, items of wealth, art, and other objects of desire rarely showed up in multiples in small towns. Raven *krawed* inside my head in obvious warning. She was uneasy about it as well. Whoever it was could just find another treasure hunter to help him out.

I pulled my draft replies folder up and found a respectful enough form letter turning down the job. Doing that always held a bit of danger, since some clients would be offended regardless, but they couldn't put a bad name out in my circles. If they did, they'd soon find their circle of friends shrink in front of their eyes. The market for my kind of talent had its own ways to ensure that those violating contracts, or worse, wouldn't find anyone willing to assist them in their dirty work ever again. I removed the auto-signature, which included my phone number, from the e-mail before pressing reply.

With at least two parties going for potentially the same thing, or at least messing around in the same area, I knew that if I had any hope of getting whatever Cody was after, I had to step up my game. It wouldn't be the first time one investigation stepped on the shoes of another in already in progress. Clues could be mixed up, evidence destroyed, scenes where things happened could get dirtied by people who had no idea that something important had happened, and of course, people's feelings got hurt.

It sounded like Cody might be getting more information from someone close to him. Maybe he'd have more clues for me soon. In the meantime, I still had the thing that had led me into this mess. I dialed Kevin's number.

"Hi Morgana, finally got some time?" he asked, his voice a little groggy. Apparently, his erratic sleeping schedule had gotten the better of him again.

"You awake enough to tell me why you called me earlier? Is it about the gold?" I asked, keeping my voice level as not to aggravate him too much.

"Yeah, hold on a moment," he said. I heard the familiar sound of coffee pouring into a cup a few moments later. A few long audible gulps later, his much more alert voice returned to the line. "Hey, yeah, I found out something quite interesting about your stone here. I have another pot brewing, so I'll be awake enough to share the details with you."

By the time we'd finished the call, he'd gone through a second pot of coffee and was making a third. Some days I hoped he would cut back, but I was afraid how he'd act if he went cold turkey. He'd been excited about the findings, but had let it slip that he'd reached out to someone on the finer details of the metal composites. I would've kicked him if he'd been in the same room, but I let it slide over the phone. That must be where Mr. McGuire had somehow gotten a whiff of what it was what we'd found. As Kevin's description of the gold continued, I become more and more sure that it was related to what Cody was after.

At one time, the rock had been a normal everyday collection of silica, carbon, various metals, and tiny amounts of sulfur. Then, slowly, from outside in, the lesser elements had begun changing into gold. The heavier elements and strain of rust that had been inside of the rock seemed to have resisted the conversion. And it had taken time. The cross-section of the rock, Kevin had said, was laced with gold inclusions, fractal patterns slowly filling the inside.

"Nature likes nothing better than replicating patterns. Minerals and metals like to clump together, though. And the conversion had started on some of the metal strands. There's no material in between, or impurities like you'd see in normal human processes of making things. Instead it's one atom of gold, followed by the next being iron. It just doesn't happen in a normal melting process," Kevin said.

I didn't like to jump to conclusions, and Kevin was incapable of it. His world was all facts and possibilities. So, he mentioned a few manufacturing techniques that might be responsible, but each would cost so much more to make the rock than merely melting it from pure gold.

And, according to Kevin, the conversion process explained the weight, or lack thereof. "You see, you still have the center of the rock essentially left alone. If I were to guess, only two fifths of the atomic weight was actually converted. There are still pockets of other metals within the gold. My guess is that they were heavy enough to avoid full conversion in the time given to it. And from that I can say that whoever started this stopped early. I don't know why, but in the area we're in there really is no shortage of magic running under our feet."

I was left with one conclusion: magic was responsible for making the rock as it was. It was a chilling thought that something in the magical world around me had such power. The alchemists of Old World had tried for generations to magically produce gold, and had gotten nowhere fast. Whoever was responsible for this lacked enough practice— or skill—to determine how long the conversion ought to take. Or they'd been interrupted before the task was done.

The last bit that Kevin shared was more practical. It seemed that some college kids had found some similar samples here and there. Since they'd tried to sell the pseudo-gold to various black market locations, the shop-keepers had kept their eyes and ears open. With each fence knowing how to evaluate proper gold, the criminals realized the weight didn't add up. The kids had finally reached out to the campus's archeology professor. Before I asked, Kevin sent me a list of addresses they'd attempted to sell the gold, and a detailed description of the area the kids said they'd found the stones. Whoever was out there apparently was practicing all over the place.

Taking a local area map, I jotted down what I believed

were some of the locations, including my own, the rocks might be from. I also put down the scene of the destruction Cody had mentioned. Sadly, there was no apparent pattern. So much for that. The good news was that at least the person trying to use the artifact seemed to have remained in the area. This would be a lot harder with a moving target. A small town with its own secrets was difficult enough to keep track of some days.

The raven was pushing me to head outside to take another look, but I knew better. Right now, I had to go over everything again, in case I'd missed anything obvious, especially with the conversation with Kevin fresh in my mind. With an annoyed *kraa,* the raven finally let go of the idea of being able to stretch its wings. I found myself a comfortable spot and focused again on the papers in front of me.

12

CODY

After talking with my grandmother, I gave my coyote the long run that he desperately craved. It felt good to let loose and chase down small animals. We ate a squirrel that didn't scurry up a tree fast enough, then napped for a while.

Now I was back in my dorm room, freshly showered and listening to my roommate watch cartoons in the common room. Sometimes, I wished I'd gotten a studio apartment, even if it was in the rougher section of town. My roomies stayed up late watching TV every night, and while they tried to be polite and lower the volume, it didn't really help with my sensitive hearing.

I'd considered my options, but most of the time I just tossed a couple pillows over my head in an attempt to block out the noise. I laid there for a while, the thoughts of the day running through my head as I tried to sleep.

Tomorrow, I had a full day of classes, starting at nine o'clock with Concepts of Physics, so I needed my rest if I wanted to function. While I wasn't horrible at the subject, I had to keep my grades up enough for my scholarships. But I couldn't stop thinking about Morgana. The tears in her eyes, regardless of how badass she was, made me wish I'd stayed a little longer to tell her it was going to be okay. Maybe I should've been a better person, and not so stuck on what I was going through.

She had more going on than just trying to find my family's talisman, and I should have respected that, but I also knew that she was probably the only one who could help me figure this out. My archeology professor had given me a wizard's e-mail address, saying he knew someone who could help, and so far he seemed right.

My phone buzzed once. I jerked upright, but the vibrations didn't continue to indicate a call. I lay back down, pissed that I was so antsy and anxious to hear back from her. Morgana had said she'd let me know when she found something out, and I couldn't expect her to move mountains in a few hours. Besides, it wasn't as if I'd gotten a lot of information from my grandmother that I could share with her. Even if I did call, she'd probably think I was being needy, and I didn't want to come across like that.

Shaking my thoughts aside, I rolled over onto my side, staring at the white wall and thinking about the first time I'd met her. I'd caught a glimpse of her naked body before she could make it around the corner, and it had turned me into a bumbling idiot. The combination of her sleek curves and the definition of her muscles awed me. It hadn't been my first time seeing a naked woman, but it was certainly the most pleasurable image I'd seen.

The television turned over to another cartoon channel, and I struggled not to listen in. If only I'd gotten some quiet guy who liked watching Netflix with headphones on, or better yet, reading in his room. But I'd have another two years to work on my selective hearing.

The phone buzzed out a steady tone, and I pushed out of bed, not wanting to get my hopes up again. A smile slid across my lips as I saw Morgana's number on the screen. It was her. I hadn't pissed her off as badly as I'd feared. Or, well, I'm pretty sure I had, but at least she was over it enough to talk with me about the job.

I sat on my bed and answered the phone. "Hey," I said.

"Hi Cody. I've been doing some digging with the information you provided, and I have some news. If you'd like to come by my place tomorrow, I'd be happy to brief you on what I've learned." Her tone was pleasant but professional.

"Great." I forced my voice to sound equally neutral, but my chest tightened, and I clenched my hand into a fist, trying not to feel the pang of rejection. She'd told me before that she wanted to keep things between us strictly business while I was her client. Probably even after, since she had hang-ups about getting into another relationship.

"Actually, it's not great. I'd like to see you tonight." My words came out quickly, prompted by a need to convince her that I was serious about this thing we might or might not have. I didn't want her just to investigate my family's lost talisman. My feelings for her went beyond that.

I forced my hands to loosen on the phone, or else I'd have to explain to my carrier how I'd managed to crush yet another one. That probably wouldn't bode well for my wallet. They hadn't really believed my explanation last time, and I think they'd made some kind of note in their system about fraud.

Morgana remained quiet for a long moment. I almost thought she'd hung up on me, and I quickly glanced at the phone to make sure the line was still connected. "I'm not sure that's such a great idea. Like I mentioned earlier, I'm just not good for relationships. But..." She sighed, and I heard the tiredness in her tone. "But I do like you. I honestly do."

The words sang in my chest. I couldn't have been happier to hear that. However, I still needed her to let herself go out on the limb and give me a chance. I wasn't like those guys she'd had in her past. At least I'm pretty sure she'd never dated a coyote before. The only problem with that was how I'd tell her. I couldn't be sure that she wasn't a human, and I'd grown up learning from my family to not spill details to others that could come back to bite me in the ass.

"Give me a chance then," I said. "Let me prove to you that you're worthy of a new relationship, even if it's just a slow and steady thing." The television in the living room switched off, and the sound of my roommate retreating to his bedroom nearly made me sigh in relief. Even if I couldn't go see her, I still had a chance of getting a good night's sleep. Maybe.

"Fine. Come over for a little bit. I might as well tell you all that I've been learning. But you shouldn't stay for long since I'm pretty tired. It's been a long day." She hung up the phone.

I threw on my clothes and grabbed a small duffel to carry them with me after I shifted. The trek to her place would take forever in my human form, but my coyote was swift and agile.

My roommate peeked his head out of his room as I entered the common area and waved a twenty at me. "Grab some more soda while you're out? You can keep the change." His family was rich, so he liked flashing money for other people to do his errands. But most of the time, I didn't mind. It put a little spending cash in my pockets.

"Sure. I don't know when I'll be back tonight, so don't wait up." I nodded to him and started to the door.

"I didn't know you had a girlfriend." He walked a little closer, chuckling with mischief. I raised an eyebrow at him, and he pointed at the duffel bag.

Yeah, I guess it did look like that. "Maybe. We're not really sure what it is yet."

"Go get 'em, tiger." He playfully punched me on the shoulder. "If I know any guy who should be able to get a girl-friend, you're it, buddy." With that, he walked back into his bedroom. I wasn't sure if that was a compliment, especially coming from him.

But I'd like to think it was. It wasn't like I was used to girls making me this antsy and needy before. Then again, there was a first time for everything.

13

MORGANA

The phone call with Cody hadn't exactly gone the way I'd planned it. I'd only thought to give him a heads up on where I was with the job and plan to get together to further inform him of what I'd learned. Him coming over now was a little much for me, even if some small part of me was somewhat glad. For the first time since Ezra's passing, I didn't feel quite so lonely.

I forced the thoughts from my head and looked out the large windowpane into the night. My eyesight was better than a human's in this form, but my eyes were at their best when I was a raven. Changing indoors was out of the question, though. My raven freaked out indoors, and even my tight control hadn't been enough the one time we'd tried it. We ended up slamming through a window and ripping ourselves to shreds. Not something I ever wanted to do again. But that had been when I'd already been upset over my parents' sudden deaths. Emotions had a way of forcing shifters to change, and ripping away their control. Now I tried to stay in the driver's seat when it came to my emotions. I didn't ever want to be that out of it ever again.

I brought my knees up to my chest on the couch and browsed the Internet on my cell phone as I waited. Tiredness made me yawn, and I laid my cheek against my knees. A sudden knock on the door had me flying off the couch to my feet. It seemed like seconds later, but the clock on my phone said differently.

I headed over to the door, brushing my hair out of my face since I hadn't really dolled up in advance of him coming over. I was kicking myself about that a little now. I didn't even have a mirror near the door to see if I had any hair sticking up all cockeyed. Damn.

I pulled open the door to see Cody standing there, a light sheen of perspiration on his forehead. He had a musky and altogether masculine scent that I wanted to sleepily curl up in. "Hello," I said. "I was almost about to call." Lie. More likely, I would've just fallen deeper asleep on my couch.

He raised his eyebrows at me. "Sorry that I woke you. I probably should've called when I got close." He reached toward me, before I knew what he was doing, and tucked a stray strand of hair behind my ear.

It took all my willpower not to lean my face into his hand. "It's okay. I'm awake now." I stepped back to let him inside, and locked the door behind him as he walked by.

He turned to me and smiled. "You sure? Point me in the direction of your coffeemaker, and I'll make us some."

I returned the smile but shook my head. "If you're looking for coffee, you're all out of luck here. I don't drink it. The best I can do is hot tea or Coke."

"No coffee?" He widened his eyes in faux shock. "Wow, I guess I am out of luck. Good thing I'm not a huge fan of it myself. I might've had to go back out to get some."

"If that were the case, I'd feel obliged to drive you." I glanced at my cell phone. "But I'm afraid you'd be out of luck, because Woodland Creek Coffeehouse is closed." I smirked at him, enjoying the bantering. It had been quite a while since I'd done that with anyone. To be doing it with him was surprising, but not unpleasantly so. Maybe I was a little harder on him than I should have been. Maybe Kevin was onto something with his advice to move on, and not waste my life on sadness, and memories of a man I'd never see again.

"Guess you're right. I'll go grab each of us a Coke?" I looked at Cody and let the thoughts of Ezra melt away. I let myself just feel for Cody, as crazy as that sounded. Maybe this was all happening for a reason, and I'd be free from all the hurt. Nodding, I smiled at him at last, happy he was here.

Cody headed into the kitchen, and I followed him. My home wasn't all that big, but it was large enough that I wouldn't want to have to yell out him, especially since I wasn't sure what his hearing was like. I still didn't know if he was a shifter, even though I kind of suspected he might be after the growl. "So, I guess I should get on with the information, since that's what you came over for."

He looked back at me with a raised brow and a slight frown on his lips. "That's not the only reason I came over. You should know that."

I stifled my smile and slid onto the barstool near the kitchen's breakfast bar. "Fine, I guess you're right. So here's what I found out."

Playing with the can of Coke, I started recounting what I'd learned from Kevin. I could see Cody's eyes glaze a little when I related his theory of the elemental conversion, but I didn't blame Cody for that. Not many got into the material sciences or material fabrication. Cody's attention was raised again as soon as I shared the detail that someone had tried to sell the stones at various merchants, and that I knew some of the areas where they'd reportedly found the stones.

"Can you show me on the map?" he asked, leaning gently toward me with genuine interest in his eyes. It had been a while since I'd seen anyone get into hunting like he was.

I brushed against him softly as I reached over to place the map between us. The touch of my skin against his was electrifying.

He gave a soft cough and leaned over the map.

"I know these areas." He pointed to two locations north of the town. "But it doesn't seem like there's a pattern here. And without a timeline of when these spots were found, I don't think we can specify exactly how things have progressed," he continued, musing over the map.

While I'd shared what Kevin had told me, I decided to keep Mr. McGuire's involvement from him. I'd turned him down after all, and I didn't want to unnerve Cody, or make him nervous that someone else might be looking for stones. Cody was my client, but he didn't need to know about other opportunities I might have. I pushed the thought out of my head and showed where I had found my piece of gold. "And there was one here as well," I said, and looked up at him.

There was a small glint of light in his eyes, and he tilted forward. "You know, all of these are along old hunting paths. These two were used for hunting deer back in the day. See how they both end up facing a cliffside? And this one here has a stream running through it, good for fishing in mid-spring. I think that we're looking for someone who's a hunter, which, sadly, out here means about half the population," he finished, his voice slowly losing its enthusiasm.

It had been there on the map all along, but somehow I'd missed it. Yes, all of the locations were perfect hunting grounds, although rarely used. "Well, at least now we have a clue to go on," I said, raising my head to look into his hungry eyes.

Cody brushed his fingers along my jawline, and I leaned into them, greedy for the tenderness in his caress. If I closed my eyes, I could remember Ezra's touch, but I also had growing feelings for Cody. He'd somehow wormed his way into my heart in much the same way Ezra had. With both men, I'd been adamant about not getting too close, already reeling from loss that had made me vulnerable emotionally. Now Cody had managed to get closer than I'd hoped.

I found it hard to care when he was this close and warm against me.

I wrapped my arms around his neck. He smiled at me and rested his large hands on my hips, as if we'd start dancing to non-existent music at any moment.

"Things are going so good. I can't imagine not having this time with you." He leaned in, and my body stiffened at the brush of his lips across mine. He hesitated, as if waiting for me to tell him that he'd done something wrong, but I couldn't. He wasn't doing anything that I didn't want him to do.

What he'd said in the car was one of the most sincere things I'd heard in a while, and I knew that he was interested in being with me because he truly wanted to be. I'd warned him of the danger, but that didn't seem to matter to him. That wasn't to say that I was about to let him get in the way when it came to my work. I wouldn't let him get hurt.

His hands ran from my hips to the small of my back, and I shivered at the sensations he brought out in me. My body savored his touch and needed more, even if I wasn't exactly sure that I was ready to have sex with him. But that didn't matter. This was what I needed. Some women went out and had one-night stands to blow off the stress of what was happening in their life. I didn't think this was a one-night stand—I hoped it wasn't—but having Cody here after I'd made some progress toward getting the destructive talisman off the streets was exactly what I needed.

He pulled me closer, pressing my body against his, so I knew exactly how happy he was to be here with me. In that moment, thoughts of anything but Cody faded away, and I leaned into him, not feeling loneliness or any other negative emotion that had haunted me for the past few months. Right now, I was who I'd always been. I was me. He made me new, and shinier than I'd been since before Ezra died.

I rose to my tiptoes and pressed a kiss to his lips, slowly at first, a matching brush of lips. He made what was almost a purring growl, and it vibrated my lips, sending more shivers up my spine. He walked me back toward the couch, and my legs bumped it, letting me know I could continue our romantic rendezvous sitting down.

I felt the vibration of my phone in my pants pocket, but I wasn't expecting any calls. I'd talked with Kevin a little while ago, and we'd squared things away. I highly doubted he'd be calling again this soon. I'd gotten a few telemarketer calls recently, so maybe it was just that. Easy enough to ignore.

He pushed me gently back onto the couch, and succeeded in brushing aside any thought of answering the phone. I felt his breath on my neck and his tongue trailed over the expanse on his way to nibble my earlobe.

I leaned my head back a little against the arm of the couch, savoring the feeling of his weight pressing me down. As I wrapped my arms around him, I felt my cell phone start vibrating again.

He pulled away from me, frowning. "I get that you're a kick-ass treasure hunter, but don't you ever get a moment for yourself without phone calls interrupting?"

I sighed and shrugged a shoulder, a little sheepishly. "Sorry. I'm not really expecting anyone to call. Let me see who it is and if they've left a message."

His frown intensified. "Really? Can't it wait?"

I leaned my head on his chest. "Fine. You're right. It can wait." But what if it was important? I doubted a telemarketer would be calling me twice in a row. I wanted to just answer it and see what the deal was, but I also didn't want to make Cody think that my work was more important than this moment. That had been one of the trigger points in my relationship with Ezra. I'd had a hard time shutting off my phone when we needed time for one another. Granted, he'd been part of my work life, as my pseudo-assistant and business manager, but I still should've learned to balance my time better.

Just as I leaned up to kiss Cody again, the phone vibrated yet again. Now I was worried. I needed to take the call. It had to be an emergency, most likely Kevin. I didn't know anyone else who would call like this.

Cody grabbed my wrist as I started to get up from the couch. "Come on."

"No, I have to take this." I pulled away from him and walked into my bedroom, closing the door behind me for some privacy. I put on some music, playing it softly to keep him from being able to listen in on the conversation if he was a shifter.

I didn't recognize the phone number on the display, but it was the one that had called all three times. "Hello?" I said, keeping my voice professional, even if I was a little anxious.

"You have some nerve rejecting me. How dare you, you silly little wretch." The man's voice held the harsh tone of authority I recognized from some of my clients. They thought that because they had a lot of money, they were superior, but they usually toned it down because they knew that without my assistance they wouldn't get what they wanted.

Still, I couldn't find my voice to reply to the man. How had he gotten my phone number? I had an email address strictly for new contacts, and yet I'd had Cody come to my house, and now this man had my phone number. I lowered myself to the floor, feeling more scared than I had in a while.

"The least you could do is respond. Face up to your consequences, because you will be feeling them. You won't reject me," he hissed the words.

"I—" Before I could say anything in return, the line disconnected, and I stared at it a moment before throwing the phone at my bed. It thumped against the mattress before falling to the floor. "Pompous asshole."

I placed my forehead against my knees, feeling absolutely sick to my stomach. How had I been stupid enough to get back into treasure hunting? I should've learned my lesson and stuck with one of the menial jobs I'd tried out in town. Or I should've kept myself from getting so wrapped up in Cody that I ignored my gut. Now I might very well be in danger because of my stupidity.

14

CODY

I clenched my hands into fists, but I kept my coyote from listening in on her conversation. Besides, she was playing music in her room, clearly to block me from even trying. How had we gone from the good fortune of her being on track to finding the talisman—and the wonderful, almost magical kissing—to being in separate rooms, with her more concerned about who was calling than being with me?

I heard a soft thump from the other room and stood. I didn't hear voices now, only the sound of the music, and I hesitated a moment. I didn't want to interrupt her, but if she was upset, I wanted to be there for her.

"Morgana?" I called, loudly enough for her to hear me, but softly enough that if she was still on the phone the other person wouldn't.

She didn't reply.

I waited for a few more moments, then walked to her room and knocked. "Morgana? Is everything all right?"

"Just go. Please." Her voice sounded a little choked, as if she was crying.

I opened the door to the bedroom and saw her sitting on the floor, her cell phone lying near the bed. Something had happened. Maybe whoever had called had given her bad news. I knelt beside her and placed a hand on her shoulder. "I'm here for you. I won't go anywhere."

She looked up at me like a wild animal, tears staining her cheeks. "No. You have to leave. I..." She looked down at the carpet. "I just need time to think. You can't be here right now. I shouldn't be so emotionally invested in you."

The way she said it made it sound like she didn't want us to be together. But that didn't make a lot of sense, since she'd been just as into making out with me as I had been. What could have changed? I glanced at the cell phone and felt jealousy flare in my chest. She'd loved and lost. But what kind of loss? Maybe she was just trying to push me away because her boyfriend might be back in the picture. Maybe he'd contacted her to try to get back in her good graces.

I rose to my feet, shaking my head. She'd been so reluctant to let me in, and maybe, just maybe, she'd been right to push me aside. It would've saved us both pain if I'd only listened to her wishes, but I'd been too pigheaded. "I should've known. How could we have had something? You're so alone and isolated out here, you just don't know how to let anyone in." I walked toward her bedroom door, but before I could get there, she threw herself in front of me.

"Wait. That's not the deal. I—"

"Save it, Morgana. I shouldn't have come over. Maybe we're just wrong for each other." Even as I said the words, they pained me more than I wanted to admit. I wanted to be with her, but my quick temper was taking over.

Her eyes widened and her mouth fell open. For a moment, I recognized that the woman I'd admired for her strength and kick-ass nature was weak, and didn't need to be kicked any further. Maybe she was reacting because of the call. Maybe it wasn't what I thought it was. But I couldn't know unless I let her get the words out.

"I'm sorry."

She closed her mouth and lifted her chin a little, the brick wall around her heart slamming back into place. "No, you're right. You shouldn't have come over. It's really just best you leave." She stepped out of my way and crossed her arms over her chest.

My heart dropped into my stomach, and I felt even worse about myself than I'd thought possible. I'd truly hurt her, and now I was really doubting my knee-jerk reaction. She was a treasure hunter who dealt with plenty of dangerous things, more than other people knew existed. How could I know she hadn't gotten a work-related call? Except... I couldn't see her reacting like this when it came to work.

Maybe she'd come around in a day or two. Maybe all she needed was some time. She was still working my job and trying to find the talisman. Besides, I'd done enough.

"Fine. I'll talk to you later, I guess." I turned and walked away. As I got closer to the door, I had a nagging feeling that something wasn't right, but my emotions were raging. I couldn't zero in on what was wrong, let alone find the energy to care. My coyote had tried talking with me about things before that didn't make sense, and I'd always listened to him. Right now, he needed to shut up and mind his own business. Until I got out of her house and away from her property, I wasn't in the mood to hear it.

15

MORGANA

I watched Cody stalk off into the darkness. He held his shoulders back, and his haughty stride made me want to punch him in the face. How could he have just blown up at me like that, when he didn't even know what the hell was going on? I couldn't believe that I'd almost let him into my life. That we'd been making out. God, how stupid was I?

I was about to close the door when my raven *krawed* at me in warning. I glanced back outside in time to see a bulky man, all in black, running at me. I slammed it shut just as he got to me, but his momentum and size made the door explode off its hinges. I flew back, sliding across the floor a couple feet, more than a little dazed. But I couldn't just lie down and let him do whatever it was he wanted to do to me. Maybe we could talk this out, and avoid violence.

"What do you want?" I yelled at him as he charged me again like a bull. I leapt out of the way, and he crashed into an end table, shattering the table and the lamp on top of it. I screamed, but I hoped Cody was far enough away that he wouldn't hear me. The last thing I needed was for him to be wrapped up in something this dangerous.

The big guy turned and looked back at me, grunting and shaking off the glass from his black suit. The only part of his face I could see well were his eyes, and what I saw in them was rage and hatred. This wasn't good at all. I looked to the files I'd had about Cody's family's talisman. Usually I locked all my files in my safe, but now I had to make the choice of leaving my house with all my things for some rhino of a man to ransack, or staying and trying to fight him.

My raven flapped her wings, wanting to go. That was the best idea, anyway. Even if I wanted to stay and fight, I couldn't go up against this guy. I was pretty good at defending myself, but a guy like him? I doubted I would even hurt him, much less do enough damage to drive him away from me and my home.

"Answer me! I don't even know what you want!" I leapt over the back of the couch as he barreled toward me again. At this rate, he was going to destroy everything in my house.

"You shouldn't have rejected my boss. He doesn't take that well, especially not from little ladies." He cracked his knuckles and threw my other lamp to the side. "You would've liked working for him, and now it just might be too late. But I'm supposed to bring you to him, so don't act dumb. If you do, I might not be able to save you from your-self and your stupid choices."

I looked toward the window, clenching my fists. There was no way I'd be able to open the door and get out of there without him getting his grubby paws on me. But I really didn't know if I wanted to break through the window again, because if I did, I might be in worse condition than if I just tried to stay and fight him. None of my options were good.

On top of that, I looked at the things smashed to pieces

to see that my picture of Ezra, the one we'd taken together in Eastern Europe, had been crumpled beneath the asshole's feet like it was trash. I wanted to pick it up and clutch it to my chest. Maybe making out with Cody had been the wrong thing to do. I couldn't help but feel like I'd betrayed Ezra. My heart fell into the pit of my stomach, and I wanted to just sob. My life was falling apart.

The thug stalked closer to me, and I took a few steps backward. I'd done all I could to distance myself from the world, and now I was surrounded by people who'd somehow found my personal information, and who I didn't want any part of dealing with. What had I done to deserve this? I'd turned clients down before, and no one had ever come after me because of it. I grabbed a candlestick from a side table and turned back toward the glass door. I swung it back, but before I could hit the pane, I was pulled back by my T-shirt and thrown to the floor.

I stared up at the big man, who had taken the candlestick from me. He lifted it up as if to hit me with it, but instead he threw it to the side. I jerked to my feet in a graceful flow of movement and lunged after the makeshift weapon, but before I could get far, pain exploded in the back of my head. I collapsed to the floor, darkness swallowing my existence.

16

CODY

I'd walked far enough into the forest that I could have some distance from her, and she wouldn't catch sight of me changing from her living room. The idea of her watching me strip just didn't do it for me right now. After that argument, all I wanted to do was punch something, but I'd settle for the next best thing: running as fast and as far as I could, and just burning off all the negative energy I was feeling. Going back there wouldn't help anything. It'd only make our tension flare that much higher, and unfortunately this tension wasn't the kind I'd been hoping for when we'd settled into the evening. My coyote wanted to feel her body pressed up against us, not have her tell us to leave and push us away the way she had. Her scent lingered inside my head, in my nose, and I found it hard not to long to smell it again.

I growled under my breath and kicked a nearby tree. It groaned a little under the assault, but I had a feeling that in the morning I'd be feeling the impact a lot more than the tree would. I patted the trunk, remembering my grandmother's teaching that all things had life in them. If that was true,

I shouldn't be taking out my anger on a tree. What the hell was wrong with me?

Leaning up against the tree trunk, I stared up into the branches. My emotions were so off-kilter that I was having a hard time recognizing myself. The full moon wasn't for a few weeks, so that wasn't the problem. I glanced back into the trees toward town. If I wanted to leave, I should be going. I stripped my shirt off, folded it, and put it in the small duffel bag I'd shoved in my back pocket while I'd been in the house with her.

I'd unbuttoned my jeans, and was just about to push them off, when my sensitive ears picked up a loud crash and a scream. I fastened my pants back up and took off toward the house, cursing myself for leaving her. This was one of the things I'd feared, and it was my fault for flying off the handle in the first place. I was stupid for believing that she was hoping to rekindle a lost love, when she'd been so warm and pliant in my arms. Why would she be there with me one moment and getting back with someone else the next minute? That made no sense.

Of course, it would've been nice if she'd actually talked to me in the first place, but it wasn't her job to assuage my ego and soothe away my surprising jealousy. Now I was afraid I'd made the biggest mistake of my life. The closer I got, the less I heard, until the soft whine of an electric motor and tires squealing down the road ripped through my ears. My heart pounded in my chest so hard I thought I was going to have a heart attack. I bent at the waist and placed my hands on my hips, staring out at the expensive tan car tearing away. I kicked at the gravel in the driveway and watched several pieces go sailing through the air. I'd fucked up big time.

How could I help her if I didn't know the first thing about why she'd been taken? I might have been able to follow the car if I'd already been in coyote form and it hadn't been going so damn fast, but by now it was pretty useless. I examined the tire tracks in the road, following them back to the house. Her front door was wide open, and I frowned, heading toward it. Maybe I could find out something if I went inside and looked around.

The door had been broken open, but the lock was still intact, so she hadn't even locked the door when the attacker had come inside. I ran my hand through my hair, self-loathing washing over me like an ice bath. Inside, it looked like a bomb had gone off in the entryway and living room. She wasn't a big girl, so I couldn't imagine how she'd been able to fend off her kidnapper for so long.

I found myself trying to get a whiff of her scent lingering in the air. A few strands of her hair, a small blood splatter, and an indentation on the wall told me that she'd defended herself despite everything. My coyote gave a small grin, which I let out to play on my lips. The trivial amount of blood meant that she was most likely alive. Arterial blood sprays were the same regardless of the prey, and they were rarely contained in small areas. No rich, deep bloody scents filled in the air. Instead it was awash with sweat and testosterone. My nose was assaulted by a barrage of unfamiliar smells, but I could pick out a few things that surprised me. One, whoever had been here had been afraid. Their anxiety was obvious in their sweat, which carried an acrid tinge of desperation. Secondly, there was the smell of someone who lingered around magic, and that slight sharpness of tin that older warehouses carried with them. I took a gander around the place and headed for the obvious target, her notes.

People rarely got kidnapped 'just because.' There was always a reason. Usually, someone the victim once worked or socialized with was involved in some fashion. While I hated violating her workspace, it was one of the better clues I had right now. My coyote wasn't too happy about it, either. His nose was turned away from the entire process, as if he was trying to avoid a future conflict. *Suit yourself. I don't have that luxury*. Her notes on the job at hand were the same as what she'd shared with me earlier, with a few details added in. None of it seemed a strong enough motive for kidnapping.

Taking in my surroundings, I turned my gaze toward the next obvious target—her computer. I wasn't familiar with all the latest and greatest in software, but the basics were the same. My skills would do, because the other option was just unacceptable. I stopped myself in the moment and realized what I was feeling. My coyote had noticed it too. I wasn't just helping someone I was interested in anymore. Instead, my intentions were those of someone protecting a person they cared about.

With a long shrug, I powered on the computer, ignoring the sense that I was violating yet another aspect of her privacy. If it would help me find her, it didn't matter. The computer had password protection enabled, and I sighed. All computers had their weaknesses, and I knew a few of them, a side benefit of playing pranks on others in the tribe. I rebooted it, and waiting patiently for a moment before I switched to booting from a secondary partition, intended for backups. A few key presses in the right place gave me a command-line terminal to the computer. There's no need for a password if what you load has none. Within a few minutes, I had complete access to her hard drive, and her files.

It didn't take long to find her e-mails. Sorting them by most recent, I started to go through the ones that stood out, and the ones she'd replied to. Nothing seemed to be relevant, until I reached an e-mail from a 'Mr. McGuire.' After reading it, the gears in my head began to turn. What was going on here?

17

MORGANA

My jaw ached from being overpowered by the man who'd attacked me. I hadn't had a chance to see his face, and all I could smell from him was desperation and some kind of musky cologne. I jerked, trying to move my arms, but it was no use—someone who knew what they were doing had tied them behind my back. A silky cloth covered my eyes. It seemed as if someone had gone to a BDSM store to purchase the tools to keep me bound and blindfolded.

I cocked my head to the side, relying on my remaining senses to examine my surroundings. To my right, something smelled sweetly metallic—the scent of blood, easy to detect, especially as a Raven shifter. I'd hunted enough to know it well. While my mundane brethren were omnivorous carrion-eaters, Raven shifters were carnivores, due to the extra energy needed to shift from human form to raven.

Drip, drip, drip. The sound came from my left, breaking through my thoughts, and I honed in it. I had to figure out where I was, using any clues I could. No obvious scent came from that direction. Could it be water? The loud plops came in a steady pattern, a few seconds between each drip.

My nerves frayed at the edges like rope coming undone, and I squirmed against my bindings, doing my best to break free. If that sound was water, it could be someone trying to clean up the blood before he left the scene. He'd probably use me for his purposes and kill me as well. *Danger.* If I didn't get out of here, I might be lying in my own pool of blood soon.

"Ah shit, it's still not coming clean. This is what I get for hiring slobs." The man's voice raised in pitch a little, belying his bravado, laying out his fear for my sensitive ears. "Stop moving around so much, girlie. Don't think I've forgotten about you, especially not after you've disrespected me." His voice deepened, and the fear disappeared, replaced by anger. "Wipe that smug look off your face, before I do it for you." He stomped in my direction.

I quickly adjusted my expression, even though it was hard. Maybe I was crazy for finding this whole situation funny, but if I didn't laugh, I'd just curl into a ball and cry uncontrollably. The smile crept back onto my lips. I tried to force it into a neutral frown, but I wasn't quick enough. The blow to my face knocked me off-balance, throwing me hard to the ground, and I lay there gasping in pain at the force behind his punch. He was human, but more than that...a wizard. *Ugh.* I could tell by the tangy scent of magic that clung to him. Plus, he was pretty damn strong.

"What do you want?" I growled between gritted teeth, hoping they were all still in my head after the blow. I remained where I was, more out of fear that he'd knock me back down than anything. My agility was beyond most, so I knew I'd be able to get up, even with my hands and arms tied behind my back as they were.

"Now you're interested." He didn't sound much older than I was, which meant he could've been a college grad with dreams far beyond his grasp. But how would he have gotten my information? "I would've thought our previous emails would strike your fancy, but I guess not. You know what to look for to get me out of my current mess. You'll give me what I've always hoped for, or you'll die trying."

Even as he spoke, I tried to remember the voice from the phone call earlier. This had to be James McGuire. Shivers of fear trailed along my spine like a cool fingertip. "If I'm going to find anything for you, you'll need to give me more information than this." I had a feeling I knew what he wanted.

"You're right. Coming to your senses. Good, I'm glad. I wouldn't want to hurt you any further than you've already forced me to." After a moment, the dripping water increased to a full-on spray.

The faint trickling sound of a small stream of water ran toward me, and I sat up, sliding away from it. The closer it got, the more I could smell the blood lacing it. I bit my lip to hold in my discomfort at the thought of sitting in someone else's blood.

The man's musky cologne closed in on me again, and I almost jerked away when he pulled both the blindfold and a few strands of hair from my head. He grabbed me by the upper arm and yanked me to my feet with such force that I nearly tripped over my own legs. I couldn't let myself underestimate him. He was stronger than I'd expected wizards could be, and I had to get over that. "Now, you'll do as I say if you don't want to get hurt."

I glanced down at his other hand and saw a long yellow garden hose traveling back toward the wall of a cabin's large shed, its walls lined with aluminum siding. Near the path to my left was a chair that he must've set the hose on while he'd gone off somewhere. That explained the dripping sound. My gaze swept to the right, and my heart dropped into the pit of my stomach.

While I'd smelled the sweet coppery scent of blood, I couldn't have imagined this view: a young woman lay on the ground in a pool of her own blood. Her hair color and style, in fact her appearance in general, was the same as mine. I bit my lip hard, but couldn't suppress a muffled scream.

He punched me again, and this time, I fell to the ground right next to the corpse. My instinct to get out of here and fly away overwhelmed me, until I felt myself beginning to change. If the shift happened, I'd be vulnerable between forms. Wizards had been known to trap shifters before they could finish the change. Looking up at him, I had a feeling that he'd do whatever it took to get what he wanted.

"Just untie me and tell me what you want." My voice trembled a little. From the corner of my eye, I saw a couple of men walking toward us. They'd come out of the cabin's side door, and they looked just as bulky and strong as the man standing before me.

"I wouldn't be that stupid. I know what you are. You're not going to get away that easily, little bird." He grabbed me by the hair and pulled me into a sitting position, making me moan in pain. "Rudy, she's seen enough. Take her upstairs. Jasper, you're cleaning this up."

I climbed to my feet before Rudy could pull me up like the first guy did. He advanced on me and I backed away a little, keeping just out of reach. "Don't touch me, Rudy. I can walk without your hands on me."

He lunged forward, but I dodged out of the way, sweeping his foot out from under him in the process. He tumbled to the floor with a loud crash, like a two-hundred-and-fifty-pound bag of potatoes.

Jasper sized me up again, as if he'd thought I was just some stupid young girl, and I'd unexpectedly impressed him. "Come on, girl. I won't touch unless you get out of line." He waved a hand out in front of him toward where I was supposed to go. "I'll fill her in and set her free like you want, Mr. McGuire."

I shuddered, anxious to get away from them. Would they actually let me go? Guess there was only one way to find out.

18

MORGANA

Jasper had been true to his word—he'd told me my job and let me walk out of the cabin—but I felt hollow and empty. The men inside were more powerful than I could fight alone. Hell, just one of them had managed to lay me out flat, so I couldn't even imagine taking them all on. If I wanted to live, and if I wanted those close to me to be safe, I needed to buck up and accept what they wanted. I couldn't really have a relationship with anyone, anyway—my work was too dangerous, and this just went to prove it. I couldn't get involved.

I kept walking until I reached the road, then walked some more. I didn't know where I was, and frankly I didn't care. If someone drove by and hit me with their car, it would've been fine. At least it would put me out of my misery. Life just wasn't pleasant for me, and it never would be. I understood that now.

Sighing, I glanced over at a group of tall trees near the side of the road. I changed direction, my raven feeling the need to spread her wings. I needed that too. Maybe it was finally time for me to gain my taste of freedom. The power that people crave. Maybe I could actually put that into reality. The idea of flying away and leaving all that I knew behind was more tempting than it should've been, but I knew that was just fantasy. I couldn't take off like that. Cody might wonder where I was, if he still cared. But what he needed most from me was to find his family's magical talisman. I'd agreed to help him, so I couldn't just turn my back on him now. However, I knew now that we couldn't be in a relationship, and I truly, truly hated that after we'd gotten so close.

I stripped out of my clothes and left them under the bushes. I didn't have anything in my pockets, so it wasn't like I really cared if I ever saw that outfit again. My raven form slid over me, and I leapt into the air, shouting out a loud *kraa* as I did so. We flew higher and higher, until we could see the town's lights in the distance. I soared toward them, knowing exactly what I needed to do. My heart wept with emotion, and the closer I got to town, the more unsteady I felt. My body exploded out of raven form, and the ground rushed up to me. I wasn't invincible—I'd die on impact, falling from such a height. Just as I got close enough to see the many cracks in the pavement, my raven form washed over me again in a flurry of feathers. Our feet tapped the ground and we pushed up into the air again, escaping near-death from emotional instability yet again.

I lifted my beak and *krawed,* slamming down the wall around my heart. If I just didn't feel, that would be better than letting myself get hurt like this. But to feel was to be human. If I tried to shut down and keep away from everyone, then I wasn't living, just surviving. Life was too damn complicated.

My home passed beneath me, and I circled to get a look at it, considering going down before I headed into town to take care of something I should've avoided to begin with. To my surprise, Cody was walking out of my front door. He shut it behind him, looking like he had to get it just right for it to fit back on the doorframe properly.

My moment of truth. I didn't want to do this, but it was the right thing to do. The only thing to do. Almost anyone in my position would, yet it felt like it could be the biggest mistake of my life. I didn't want Cody to be the one that got away—or more accurately, the one I really liked but pushed away. But that was how it had to go. I couldn't be responsible for him getting hurt or killed. I wouldn't be able to live with myself. Maybe at that point, I would fly into the sky and just let myself fall.

Even as I thought that, my raven *krawed* at me. She thought I was a coward and weak. Cowards did things like that. We weren't weak or cowards. We wouldn't let ourselves do such a thing, not when we had the potential for so much more. Those thoughts were probably her survival instinct trying to cheer me up, but I knew I wouldn't stoop to that level anyway.

I would take care of what needed to be done. Perhaps then I'd be off to another destination, away from my perfect paradise, with its silly annual Demon Run coming up, and all the goofy pranks many wouldn't expect from a town with people capable of magic and mayhem.

I dipped lower to the ground, and when I was about a foot away from the grass near the gravel driveway, I shifted into my human form.

Cody had been watching my raven form with a stern curiosity. His heartbeat was racing, but when I shifted my form, a weight seemed to be lifted from his shoulders and relief lightened his expression. He ran to me, and I put up my arms, a little freaked out. The last person who ran at me had been trying to kill me. But I knew he was just happy to see me. He'd never hurt me on purpose. Not like I was about to do to him.

"You're here. You're...alive!" Sighing, he wrapped his arms around me, burying his face into my shoulder. "God, I was so scared. What happened? Are you all right?"

I let my arms hang down at my sides, and bit my lip as tears caressed my cheeks. Why did he have to do this? Why did he need to cause such feelings in me? I didn't want to have to do this, but it was for the best, for both of us.

"I..." My throat was raspy and kind of sore, probably from the screaming earlier. "We need to talk."

19

CODY

I pulled back a little. To say I was worried was a vast understatement. First she'd been kidnapped right out from under me, and now she was back. Why had they let her go? Had she managed to escape? It didn't make any sense that she was here. Her cabin was the first place someone would look for her.

"What's wrong?" I said slowly. Carefully. From the look on her face, I didn't think this was a conversation I wanted to have with her, but I supposed I needed to know where her head was at.

She nodded toward the house. "It's cold. I...I should get inside." Without another word, she turned away from me, and while I enjoyed looking at her body, I couldn't say I took a lot of pleasure in it right now. I was still worried about her, and she had bruises sprinkled all over her. I looked back at the road, where the tire tracks still glared at me. I should just go and try to find out what I could. Maybe I could find who had taken her and get some justice, since she didn't seem to be particularly into that herself right now.

I didn't think going to the police would be our best

option, not until I knew what was going on with her. Her shoulders were slumped forward dejectedly, and she was holding herself like she'd given up. I wanted to put my arm around her shoulder, but she didn't seem very receptive to that at the moment.

I carefully opened the door for her, making sure not to damage it further. Once she was inside, I set it carefully back on the frame and locked it to keep it in place. Not that it'd do too much good if whoever had broken down her door decided to come back.

She walked to her bedroom, and I hung back a little, letting her do what she needed to do. I heard the shower start, and I grimaced. Looked like I'd be hanging out for the moment, left wondering what was going on. On the kitchen counter was a closed laptop, with a set of papers next to it. I was trying not to snoop into her things, so I'd kept myself mostly away from it before, but now I wondered whether that was the right decision, for her sake. I walked closer to better inspect it. The envelope had my name on it, and I opened the folder to see general information about me and my family. There were pictures of me and my family members, my birth certificate, and my mother's passport information.

I wondered for a moment if maybe those people had taken her because of the commotion the golden rocks had created. Could they be after my family's talisman?

Anger burned in my veins, and I let out a low growl.

"What are you doing?" Morgana asked.

I looked up at her, just then realizing the water had stopped. She was dressed in yoga pants and a tank top, with a towel covering her black hair. "You... Sorry. I saw my name on it, and I..."

"It's fine. We talked about most of what's in there already, but that's not what I wanted to discuss right now." She wrapped her arms around her waist as if she was still cold. "I...I mentioned it before, but we really can't be together. My job is too dangerous for relationships." She spread her arms out in front of her. "I really like you, but it's just not possible. Not now, and not ever. Sooner or later, someone with a grudge will come along, and they'll have a way to get to me...you."

She rubbed her hands over her arms and shook her head. "I can't have that on my conscience. You mean a lot to me, and I've already had too much death and loss for a life-time. My previous boyfriend died while we were treasure hunting in South America. My parents died because of a 'mysterious' car accident when I was younger. My dad was also a treasure hunter. It's in my blood, but I'm pretty damn sure that the accident wasn't mysterious. It was someone getting even."

My legs weakened a little, and I leaned back against the kitchen counter. Here I'd been so quick to think poorly of her, imagining that she'd faced loss in the form of being dumped. It hadn't even occurred to me to think death. Now I knew why she'd been hell-bent on keeping me at a distance. But I couldn't let her push me away, not when she seemed to need someone else to stand alongside her. She looked so hopeless, and the bruises... I couldn't just leave her alone. Not even if she told me to.

"I can't give my job up, especially not now." She let out a sigh and looked up toward the ceiling. "I have too much riding on me. Something has to give, and whether I like it or not, it has to be us."

Pushing off the counter, I growled, but not at her, more out of the building frustration that ate at me. She just looked at me like she was trying to figure me out, not like she was scared. Then again, after the mess that was her house, I didn't think she was going to scare easily.

"No, I can't let you push me away. I can't, babe." I crossed the space between us and wrapped my arms around her. "We can handle this together. You need someone to be there for you. You can't be alone in this forever. You could be hurt. I'm sorry about your parents and your boyfriend, but I'm not like either of them. I'm...not human. I'm like you." I shifted on my feet, not really comfortable with doing this, but she'd shown me her form, both human and bird shifter, and I should give her the same.

Without any more words, I pulled my shirt off and slid my hands to my jeans, unfastening them with a few jerky moves. She placed her hand on my chest, stopping me for a moment. Her eyes were a little uncertain, as if she wasn't quite sure what to think of what I was doing. But after a moment she pulled away again, letting me continue. My pants dropped to the floor, and I had a moment to see her surprised, if not rather lusty, reaction to my naked body before I shifted to my coyote form. She slid to her knees so she was face to face with me. My coyote was more the size of a grey wolf than a normal coyote.

"Wow." She looked me over, but I noticed that she didn't look me directly in the eyes in this form. She was smart, and had obviously been around enough predators to know better. Not that she wasn't a predator too, but birds weren't exactly the highest on the food chain. She leaned her face into my neck after a moment, and I sat down, letting her run her hands over my fur. "I didn't think you were a shifter. You seemed like a nice, simple college guy. Except for the growl, of course, but I don't know... I chalked it up to not hearing you properly or something. I don't know what I was thinking, and I honestly still don't know what to think." She pulled back a little. "These people who are after me... They're scary. I...I've never encountered anyone like them, and I never want to again. They want me to retrieve an artifact for them, and..." She lowered her head and shook it, as if she'd said all she would.

I shifted back to my human form, heedless of the fact I'd be naked when I did. I didn't care. I needed to talk with her and console her. She needed to know my hunch, even if I was entirely wrong about it, and I needed to know more about what the people who'd kidnapped her wanted her to retrieve. Maybe they'd given her more specifics that she hadn't yet shared with me, that would prove me wrong. I hoped like hell that was true.

She stared at me, her gaze sweeping over my body, even as she tried to keep her eyes from between my legs. She wasn't doing a good job of that, either. A rosy blush tinted her cheeks, and she nibbled her lower lip before finally meeting my eyes again.

"Like what you see?" I asked, smirking at her as her blush intensified.

"Uh, yeah. Sure." She grabbed my jeans from beside us and tossed them at my lap, effectively covering me up, for the most part. But I could tell she'd been a little reluctant to do it. Her gaze still slid to my chest for a few moments before she seemed to catch herself and yanked it back up to my eyes. "Um..."

Seeing how flustered she was at my nakedness nearly made me forget why I'd changed back to my human form. Right. We needed to talk.

I leaned in a little closer to her and brushed my fingertips over her cheek. "I can help you. Tell me what kind of artifact they want."

She leaned into my chest and wrapped her arms around

me. Her small hands on my bare skin caused blood to pool in my dick, but now would be the worst time for an erection, especially since I bet she'd notice, given how close she was to me.

"They told me a little bit about it, and I'm nervous about what it might be." She looked up into my eyes as if begging me to understand.

"You're afraid it might be my family's talisman?"

She pressed her cheek against my chest and nodded. "Yeah. Their descriptions and the things you've told me about it match."

I ran my hand over her back in soothing circles. I no longer needed to be concerned about the erection. It was all gone now. While I'd had a hunch about it being my family's talisman, I hated that I'd been right. If Morgana's kidnapper jerk knew it existed after the recent magic damage in the woods, how many other people might also know about it? I clenched my free hand into a fist and leaned my forehead against the top of Morgana's head.

"We'll get this sorted out. You can count on me. Just give me a chance, babe. That's the only thing I've wanted."

20

MORGANA

After seeing Cody's massive coyote form, I didn't doubt that he'd be able to handle himself in a fight. But I still worried about him getting hurt. Even as a Raven shifter I'd gotten myself into places that almost killed me. In fact, it'd happened twice so far tonight. I didn't want his blood to be on my hands, but I also had to accept his help right now, since I seriously didn't know how else I'd get myself out of this mess.

"Okay. Just promise me you won't put yourself in needless danger." I glanced up at him, savoring the firmness of his warm chest beneath me. Being held in his arms gave me a strength that I'd desperately needed, something I hadn't been aware I lacked before now.

"I promise." He squeezed me a little tighter for a moment, and I bit my lower lip at the sight of his muscles flexing.

Whew... He needed to get dressed before I stripped away the jeans that lay across his lap and continued what we started earlier. Need flared inside me, but now wasn't the time. Not with bad guys breathing down my neck. If they knew Cody was here, and that he was important to me, they'd use him for leverage to make sure I did what they wanted.

"Good. I guess we need to get busy." I pulled away from Cody and climbed to my feet. My gaze landed on the wreckage of my home, really taking it in in the dawn's light. My stomach roiled, and I leaned back against the wall, placing my hands on my belly. "God, he destroyed my home." I couldn't keep the torrent of emotions that flooded me out of my voice. "It's..." I shook my head and looked up at the ceiling, only to see a few shards of glass from the lamp embedded there.

Cody pulled me into his arms again. This time I didn't care that he was naked. I just needed his warm body against mine. "We'll clean it up. It'll be okay. I promise." He cupped my chin in his hands and forced me to look at him. His eyes held an angry confidence, and I actually believed him. "Where should we start? You know better than I do what's going on. How will we find the talisman?"

I sucked in a deep breath and held it for a moment before letting it out slowly. He was right. I needed to focus on the task at hand. "Let's look at the map of where the last instances of magic were. I think we should head out and visit them. They've all been in a relatively small radius, and none of them have left the forest, so if we look long and hard enough, we should be able to find it. I'll be able to scout from the air, and perhaps you can scope out the scents on the ground to see if they're any help."

I stood up a little straighter, feeling better now that we were making a plan, a way to fix the damage and both get to a place where we were safe. "First though, I want to pay a visit to my wizard friend Kevin. He was looking at the first golden rock I found, and he's been keeping tabs on where they've been spotted, since he has more local contacts than I do. If we're able to see the most recent sighting of these rocks, perhaps we'll find a better lead than if I just fly around the whole forest." I gave him a half-smile, and he returned it with a soft kiss on my lips.

"All right. That sounds like a plan. I'll follow your lead." With that, he shifted back into his massive coyote form and nuzzled my thigh.

The wet touch widened my eyes, but I couldn't help laughing, before heading toward the sliding glass door. It would be easier for me to just open it and let us out instead of trying to mess with the front door. He had a mischievous look on his face, and his tongue hung out to the side like he was laughing with me. Once I'd opened the door, I waved him through with a slight bow, and he licked my face before strolling outside.

Blinking and looking after him, I wished we could spend more time together before we ventured out into the woods and dealt with this crazy mess. The more time I spent with him, the more I wanted him as a solid part of my life. I could see where my feelings for him might even eclipse what I'd had for Ezra. While I'd loved Ezra, he'd been human and never really understood the shifter part of me. That and him thinking I worked too much... But that had ended up being his downfall. My work.

Closing the glass door behind me, I locked it, storing the key under one of the smaller potted plants. Then I shrugged out of my clothes and looked up to see Cody sitting and watching me. He didn't have the laughing, mischievous look on his face anymore. He was serious and intent on me. I bit my lower lip, and he slid his tongue across his muzzle as if reacting to that gesture.

My heartbeat pounded in my chest, and I let my raven form slide over me before I could throw myself on the ground and spread my legs for him. Not now. Not yet. Soon enough we'd be able to experience that together, but right now, we had other problems to deal with.

We flapped our wings, and I launched myself into the air. I didn't go quite as high as I normally did, not only because of my previous near-death experience. I needed to stay in range so Cody could keep an eye on me. If he couldn't see me, we'd get split up, and this would all take much longer than it needed to. Granted, once we'd visited Kevin, we might have to split up anyway, depending on what he said. While it was great to stick together to track down a crazy person in the forest, it was also impractical. But we could discuss where we'd meet up when we came to that.

I only hoped Cody had good stamina since he'd need it with all the travel we were going to be doing. At least I could let the wind carry me as I glided through the air.

We traveled through the forest together for a while. I kind of enjoyed not being so detached from everyone else, at least having Cody there with me. He'd kept up just fine so far. For such a large coyote, he was pretty darn quick.

I couldn't help being impressed by him as he ran below me. My raven *krawed* at me, and I glanced up in time to see a tree coming straight at us. We twisted to the side, barely dodging it. Ugh. *Keep your head on the task at hand. Not implanted into a tree as you're flying.*

After several minutes, we finally made it to the area near Kevin's cabin. Like me, he wasn't comfortable being too close to people. Then again, with all of the magical experiments he performed, that made sense. He wouldn't want a magical explosion to set a neighborhood on fire, or for people to get into his business and call the fire department or police on him as a suspected drug cook.

The raven *krawed* at Cody for me as we slowed down a little, coming closer to the ground. Having him right behind me made me feel a little nervous. Maybe because, while I trusted him, he was still a huge coyote and I was a raven. He could rip me to shreds in this form without much effort, or just trample me. But he was good about keeping a safe distance between us.

While I allowed the shift into human form to run its course, I took the time to look around. Cody was still in his coyote form, which was probably just as well. Both of us walking up to Kevin's naked would be a sight. At least Kevin was more or less used to me showing up like this. Well, maybe less, but I didn't really have any other options.

Heading toward the cabin, I was startled by Cody's bark. He nudged something on the ground in front of him with his nose. His shirt. He hadn't been wearing it when I saw him earlier. Maybe he'd dropped it while he was outside and had the forethought to grab it again.

I knelt in front of him and pressed a kiss to the tip of his nose. "Thanks." He licked my lips, and I grabbed the shirt as a trickle of desire slid over me. God, I was so not into bestiality, but Cody seemed to have such a profound effect on my body that it didn't matter what form he was in, he still made me needy and wanton.

I slid the t-shirt over my head, and it fell to the tops of my thigh. Brushing off the leaves, I climbed the porch stairs and stopped in front of Kevin's front door, listening carefully. The place was completely silent. He might be asleep, but I kind of doubted that. There would at least be some level of noise coming from the house. Something. But maybe I was wrong. Maybe Kevin didn't snore anymore.

I knocked, but as I did, the door slid open. My heart dropped into the pit of my stomach and nausea welled up inside me. He would never do that. He had a lot of valuable lab equipment downstairs. He always kept the house locked up tight. I pushed open the door, and Cody nudged me out of the way. There wasn't much I could do about that, since he was much bigger than I was.

He sniffed around, walking slowly but steadily toward the basement. I wanted to shove him out of my way and go check the house, but I also wasn't sure if anyone else was there right now, and he was the more formidable of the two of us. My best plan of attack would be to escape, but he could actually take on whoever might be waiting to jump out at us. Still, I didn't want him to risk himself needlessly, and I was really concerned about Kevin. This wasn't like him. I wondered if somehow the bad guys had heard through their grapevine that he was involved with me.

I pressed my palms hard against my face, then ran my hands through my hair. *Okay, calm down.* I couldn't let my emotions get the best of me again. That'd only lead to chaos.

Cody pressed forward, faster now, headed to Kevin's bedroom. Things were thrown everywhere. While I knew Kevin was super neat in his lab, I'd never really had need to come into his room before, so some of this might be clutter, but the broken and slightly smoldering objects were definitely not normal, though. It was reminiscent of my home after I was attacked, except Kevin hadn't had as much time to react. He'd probably been sleeping when it happened.

I turned and ran to the basement, determined to see what they'd done to his lab. He'd had the golden rock there, among other things. Had they taken it? When I got to the bottom of the stairs and flipped on the light, my heart hammered in my chest. The lab was completely destroyed, as if someone had come in and just broken everything purposefully, rather than it just having been collateral damage from a fight.

On the wall, in something that looked like blood but wasn't, judging by the smell, was written '*find the artifact, or your wizard friend will pay with his life...as will your boyfriend.*'

Sitting on the steps, I pressed my face against my naked legs. *Keep calm. They won't kill him, not yet.* However, I knew that they would be willing to. I'd already seen one dead body tonight, and I didn't need to add two more to that number.

Cody barked at me, and I looked up to him. He jerked his head very deliberately, as if trying to tell me to follow him. I nodded and rose to my feet, a little unsteadily. I clutched the stair rail tight to keep from tumbling down to the basement again.

He remained at the top of the steps until I was right there next to him. He nuzzled me softly, then walked back to the bedroom, with me following close behind. I didn't want to come back in here—it was another reminder of how dangerous I was to those who tried to get too close—but I knew he'd probably found something important. He transformed into his human shape, and I wrapped my arms around him, needing the hug. He held me for a long moment.

"It's going to be okay. You said you trusted me. We'll make this right. We'll get your friend back, I swear." He ran his hand over my back, and I let out a shaky breath.

"If we don't, they'll kill him." I looked up at him with tears in my eyes. "They murdered a girl who looked like me and left her right there for me to see. Maybe they'd taken her mistakenly, and..." I opened my mouth to keep speaking, but I didn't even know what else to say. I shook my head and pressed my forehead against his chest. "I do trust you. I just don't want us or anyone else to die by their hands."

21

CODY

I hated seeing Morgana like this. She was a strong and independent chick who kept turning me down—now she almost seemed broken. I wanted to help her put her pieces back in place, but I didn't even know where the glue was. Then again, maybe some of that kick-ass attitude had been a front to cover up all her pain from the death and misery she'd gone through in her life.

Pulling her close just to hold her for a moment, I surveyed the disaster around us. She needed the hug, but I also needed to tell her about what I'd found. There'd been a stack of papers under the bed that looked like someone had thrown them there in a hurry. They were spread all over, but I'd managed to get them somewhat organized without putting too many bite marks in them.

"I want to show you something." I pulled away from her a little, not wanting to let go entirely just in case her knees gave out on her. After seeing how unsteady she'd been on the stairs, I didn't want her to fall and hurt herself. "These were under the bed." I bent to the stack I'd laid on the bed and picked them up, handing them to her.

She flipped through them, and a frown creased her brow.

"What?"

The frown increased as she kept flipping. "It seems like the golden rocks stopped somewhere near here. He had a few ideas why, and he marked the spot, so we should be able to find it." She dropped to her knees on the floor before me, and I took a shallow breath, but she glanced under the bed and grabbed an envelope that I'd missed. It had her name on it. She looked up at me, and sadness crept into her eyes again. "This must've been how he knew to connect Kevin with me. God, if only I hadn't dragged him into helping me, he might be fine."

I knelt beside her. "Stop beating yourself up. There's no way you could've known that they would come here to Kevin."

"The guy's also a wizard, so it makes sense that he'd know Kevin was involved in this kind of work too. Maybe when I rejected him, he came to see Kevin and found out something about us working together." She jumped to her feet, not seeming to have a problem walking now. In fact, she jogged into the living room, poking around as if she knew about something I didn't. Frowning at her, I followed, giving her space but ready to help her when or if she needed me to.

She picked up a picture of her, Kevin, and another guy, presumably her dead boyfriend, from an end table. It would be obvious enough for someone who was trained to pay attention to their surroundings. They were all smiling and had their arms wrapped around one another, on a white sandy beach with a clear blue ocean behind them.

I wrapped my arms around her waist and rested my chin on her shoulder. She let out a soft sigh and placed her hand on mine. "This must've been a clue. At least we know what's at stake." She set it back down on the table, then turned in my arms and pressed a soft kiss to my lips. "Let's head to the spot he wanted to tell me about. Kevin was smart. I think we'll find something important there."

I pressed another kiss to her lips before pulling away from her. "Lead the way. You're more familiar with this part of the woods than I am."

She smiled, then stripped off my shirt and handed it to me before brushing past me on her way out the door. I watched her body shrink and feathers sprout from her skin. It was mesmerizing to watch how effortless her change was. I shook the thoughts from my head as she *krawed* at me, cocking her head to the side in that unusual, birdlike manner.

I let my coyote come over me, grabbed the shirt between my teeth, and took off after her.

We traveled for a while, but it didn't feel nearly as long as it should've been from the map. Maybe I was more into the running than I'd thought. Looking up at her distracted me a little, but I mostly kept my gaze straight in front of me, letting the coyote have his chance to really run and let out all the aggression and frustration we'd both been feeling the last few days. I didn't know how else to deal with it. Except have sex, but I didn't want to force myself on Morgana, even though I knew her body was as willing and aroused at the possibility of us consummating our relationship as I was.

But first things first. We needed to survive long enough for that to be an option.

22

MORGANA

I looked over the area, matching the features I saw to the ones on the map. We should be close to where the last golden rock was found, but as hard as I looked, I didn't see anything or anyone. However, the cloying scent of decay caressed my nose, and the carrion-eater in me zeroed in on the scent. I flew in the direction of the smell, hovering over a large boulder for a moment before gently touching down. Only then did I notice the strange gold tint to it. My raven *krawed* at the shiny object, and we hopped over to the back side of it. A very pale and slightly wrinkled form lay on the ground. His long black hair looked Native American, but he seemed too ancient to be the one causing all this trouble.

Cody entered the clearing and sniffed the air. He saw me on the boulder and walked around to get a better view of what I was looking at. When he saw the body, he stopped, and a mournful howl rose from his throat. His coyote form melted away, and he crawled to the corpse on his hands and knees. I leapt from my spot to be near him if he needed me, but I didn't understand what was going on.

Then it hit me. This must've been someone Cody was

related to. I shifted back to human and waited nearby, hoping to be a warm presence in his darkness.

"Jacy... How could you have done this?" he whispered. "Why?" He slid his fingers carefully over the corpse's open, frightened eyes, closing them. He cleared his throat, his voice choked with tears. "This is my cousin. I can't leave him here like this. I have to take him home before the wild animals decide to eat him."

"Do you want me to come with you?" While I wanted to get this all done and over with as soon as I could, there was no way I'd leave him to deal with his grief alone. He and his cousin had obviously been close.

He glanced over at me and sighed. "I'd like that. My shirt is over by the boulder." He lowered his gaze back to the body and shook his head. "I never thought he'd be the one behind this. I should've seen it, though. He'd been different recently. Not at all like the best friend I'd had since childhood." Cody lifted his cousin into his arms carefully, and my heart ached for him. I hadn't been strong enough to take Ezra out of the cavern we'd been in when the trap had sprung on us. We'd been fighting again, and he hadn't been paying close enough attention to where he was walking...

Ugh, not the time for that.

I grabbed Cody's shirt, sliding it over my head. We walked side by side, the scent of impending rain and his dead cousin filling the air. I placed my hand on his upper arm and gave him a comforting smile.

He sighed, but smiled back weakly. We both had reasons for wanting this asshole wizard dead. While Cody was mourning his cousin for getting involved, I frowned as a sudden thought struck me. Wait, where had the talisman been? Had we missed it?

I darted back through to the clearing again and searched

around the slightly tinted rock. There was no sign of the talisman anywhere. Instant disgust snapped inside me— maybe they'd taken the talisman in addition to Kevin. But that didn't make any sense. They'd wanted me to find it, and they even said that on the wall. They hadn't been able to locate it themselves. Unless it was still around here, or on Cody's cousin somewhere. I knelt to see if it had fallen from Jacy's hand when he'd died, and that made me think.

Cody walked back to where I was. "What's wrong?" He frowned down at me.

"The talisman. I don't see it anywhere." My eyes rose to his cousin, and I saw that his hands were clenched tightly, as if he was holding onto something.

Cody looked down, following my gaze. He gently set his cousin to the ground again and examined his closed hands. "It's there, but I'm afraid of breaking his fingers if I try to remove it."

I'd had a little too much experience with doing this, even for my own liking, but when you're regularly faced with prying treasure from mummies' fists, you learn to do what you have to do.

"May I?" I took a step forward, and he nodded, although he looked a little reluctant to let me mess with his cousin's hand. "I promise I'll be gentle with him."

"I know."

I pinched the end of the talisman with my fingertips and wriggled it a little, doing my best to keep from moving enough to damage his hand. It was difficult, especially in the almost mummy-like condition his body was in. After a few minutes it finally slid free, and I let out a sigh of relief. The talisman was smaller than I'd expected, carved out of a dark, heavy wood. The odd-looking figurine had a man's legs and those of various other animals merged together to form the body of a figure sitting in a meditative pose.

My hand burned as I held it, and I dropped it to the ground, looking down at the red spot where it had touched my skin. Cody leaned in to look at my hand in the morning light, and pressed a kiss to it. "It should heal fairly quickly," he said.

"Thanks. I didn't anticipate it doing that."

"It's mindful of who it allows to hold it." He looked down at his cousin. "Maybe that's one of the reasons Jacy succumbed to it. He must have used it far too much for his safety. He shouldn't have done this. He should've known just how powerful the damn thing is." Cody shook his head and picked the talisman up. It seemed to glow a little in his grasp, and I blinked at it in amazement. "Let's get him to my grandmother's house so we can get back to dealing with those sorry bastards who hurt you."

I nodded, not knowing what else to say. Cody was feeling the pain of the situation as much as I was, and I hated seeing him hurt like this. I loved his silly, grinning coyote, and his college boy side, who was a little too eager to convince me to help him. I followed him, letting chirping birds and the morning breeze fill the silence alone.

23

CODY

Jacy's body lay in my arms. I really regretted that I had to present my grandmother with the news that he was dead. It seemed like he'd been using way too much power too quickly. From the looks of it, he was trying to turn the boulder into another golden rock. While Morgana had mentioned that the golden stones had been getting purer and purer in quality, it seemed like an awful big leap to go from smaller chunks of rock to an honest-to-God boulder.

The more I thought about it, the more I wondered what had possessed him to do such a thing. Had he been coerced by the wizard who'd been responsible for ordering Morgana's kidnapping? That didn't quite make sense. I looked over my shoulder at her. She was watching our surroundings, her gaze scanning the forest as if expecting the enemy to jump out at us at any time.

I didn't blame her. I was keeping an eye out too. While I knew that the area near the forest where my grandmother lived was pretty secure—no one was stupid enough to cross her totems and the magical repellent she'd laid out—I knew these people were willing to do whatever it took to get what they wanted.

By the time we got to her house, the positioning of the sun told me it was nearly noon. My feet were kind of sore from stepping on all the little rocks and twigs on the forest floor. I caught the slightest bit of a limp from Morgana, but she kept her chin up and didn't say a word about it. She just soldiered on.

The door to the house opened, revealing my grand-mother leaning against the doorframe. "I welcome the follower of the Raven back into the lands that once were. Welcome, daughter of the skies. I had hoped that we'd have a chance to meet at a different time, but adversities bring out who we really are, I suppose. Come over here so that I can have a better look at you," she said, her voice carrying easily across the distance between us.

Morgana didn't seem fazed by her words as she made her way up the steps to the doorway. "Hello, Wise One. I think I'm somewhat responsible for what is going on," she began, but was quickly silenced by a wave of my grand-mother's hand.

"Don't fret. The spirits have been more than clear about it. Jacy is with them now, and he already knows what he'd brought upon us. There is no need for hostility, just accep-tance. Do come in," Grandmother moved out of the way, deeper into the house. Not wanting to make her wait, I walked in after Morgana, closing the door behind us. The air felt different, heavy with emotion and isolation. It seemed that Jacy's passing, and how it had occurred, had hit my grandmother harder than I'd expected. There were whispers in the air, barely audible to my ears. I couldn't pick any meaning out of them, but I could tell that the spirits were close to us.

"May I see it, Cody?" she asked, her voice tremulous with emotion.

I retrieved the talisman and let her have a good look at it. There was a glint of sadness, but also anger, in her eyes as she held the talisman at arm's length, peering into it at something I couldn't see. With a nod, she retrieved the pipe and blew a small portion of the smoke close to the talisman, appeasing whatever was trapped inside. Emotion left the surface of the magical figurine, and the air got slightly lighter afterward. Whatever the talisman was capable of in addition to changing materials to gold and spawning tornadoes, I didn't want to know.

It had already brought ruin to someone in my family because of greed. The more I looked at the innocent-looking sculpture, the more I was certain that it was evil. And those who had been exposed to it in greed or lust for gold were more than likely to meet their untimely ends.

"I'm sorry, Grandson. I'll have to ask you to carry it a bit further. I must not touch it, for it would burn my hands. Your uncle will take care of it when he comes here tomorrow. Until then, you need to keep it close," my grandmother said, and locked her eyes onto mine.

Unable to refuse, I nodded, feeling displeasure grow from within the talisman. "Now, you two can't go out quite as you are. I may still have something of yours. Raven, could you help me?" She walked toward the back of the house without waiting for a reply from Morgana.

I waited out in the living room while Morgana and my grandmother talked quietly in the back room, searching for something. Occasionally I heard faint, half-contained laughter from the back, but with all the spirits pushing to break into our world, I wasn't sure if it was actually them. Ten minutes later Morgana returned wearing my old middle-school clothes. The band on the t-shirt had long ago broken up, and the colors on the jeans had faded. She carried a stack of other clothes with her, and I felt my heart sink a little. I knew that the only other clothes here that would fit me would be from when I was in high school. Sure enough, I found a black heavy-metal shirt I'd worn to school and a pair of ripped jeans among other similar ones. Ones I thought I'd given away.

"You've done well to ally yourself with the Raven, Grandson." My grandmother nodded at me. Sadness wrinkled her face even more, and her shoulders seemed more slumped as she walked back inside her home.

I wrapped my arms around Morgana, needing to feel her life and warmth. She held me gently, letting me lean forward to rest my chin on her shoulder. I wanted to cry and yell and fight, but I had to remain cool and calm. I had to let the coyote take his revenge for what happened to my cousin, and to Morgana. I slid my finger lightly over a bruise that marred her light complexion, and stood up straighter, pushing my shoulders back.

"Do you think you can find the place they took you again?"

She bit her lower lip doubtfully. "Um... I didn't really pay as much attention to where I was going as I should have. I think I can find my way back though. I was flying higher up in the air than I probably should've been at the time, but retracing my path is worth a shot. We'd have to go back to my house first, so I can go back to the last waypoint that I remember."

I nodded. "Yeah, that's not a problem." I looked at the keys to my grandmother's truck in my hand. "It'll probably be quicker for you to fly to where McGuire normally is, but maybe we could drive back to your place?"

She nodded quickly, and I could see the relief in her eyes. Morgana hadn't wanted to travel back like that any more than I did.

I opened the passenger door of the truck to let her in. I caught sight of her feet as the flip flops my grandmother had given her came away from the bottom of her foot. Her feet were bruised and red. It looked like they'd been bleeding. Her healing speed must've stopped them from getting worse, but it wasn't enough to make the bruises go away.

She must've caught me looking, because she pulled her leg quickly into the truck and placed her feet flat on the floorboard.

"I'm fine. I swear." She leaned up to kiss me, and the feeling of it brought a level of relief that I hadn't realized I'd needed. Her hand trailed over the thin shirt, snug on my skin now that I filled it out better than in high school. I couldn't believe my grandmother still had some of my clothes, but I guess she'd never gotten around to donating them.

I'd lived with her mostly in my high school years. Not only did she live closer to the high school, but after I'd shown signs of being more than human, she'd been more understanding than my own family. I'd already been different, and my being a Coyote shifter made me even more of an outcast.

I brushed the thoughts away as Morgana's face filled with concern, and closed the door to head over to the driver's side. I didn't really want to talk about my childhood with Morgana, at least not yet. But from what I had seen of the files in her living room, I could tell that she'd done her research well. I hadn't had time to go through all of it, but she knew more about me than anyone I had ever met, maybe even as much as my closest family members.

I slid into the driver's seat and started the engine. We drove to her house with only the sound of older country music on the radio to break the silence. I knew not to change it away from the station. My grandmother had a way of knowing things. Besides, I didn't really mind it. The music filled the gap between us, so I didn't feel like I had to talk about what was bothering me.

Morgana didn't seem to feel the need to either, and I liked that about her. We could just be here in a companionable silence. There was no pressure to do anything else.

I pulled into her gravel driveway, right beside the garage, where tire tracks still gouged the driveway. When I cut the engine, I looked over at her, and she was staring out the front window. She didn't look anxious to get out of the truck.

"Do you think that we'll be able to fight them all? I know you're also a big coyote, but the guy who attacked me and kidnapped me was huge, and strong. I... You saw my living room. I just don't know how we'll be able to take them on alone." She sighed and leaned her head back against the headrest. "I'm not saying we won't, but it'll be tough, and we're both already kind of tired from all the walking earlier."

"We'll do it. We...you...have what they want, and they won't know I'm there." I laid my hand on hers. "Let's play into what they think will happen. They know you're scared, and that you'll give them the talisman. They don't know you have help. If we can keep them believing that for a moment, then I can jump out when things start happening, and we'll have the element of surprise."

I held up another talisman my grandmother had slipped into the pocket of the jeans she'd given me. "You can give them this one and I'll hold onto the real talisman."

"What if they realize it's not the real one? I'm pretty sure a wizard would know the difference." Frowning, she turned to look at me, and drew in a breath before letting it out slowly. "I'm not doubting you. I just want to be prepared in case things go downhill. I don't want them to catch us off-guard."

She was right, of course. I didn't know if the wizard would be able to tell between the two. He obviously knew what the real talisman did, but could he sense the magic in one versus the lack of it in the other? It made sense that he might. If that was the case, then I didn't want to be throwing Morgana to the wolves. We needed to have a better plan than this. "You're right. I don't know if he'll be able to tell the difference. We should be prepared, just in case."

She rubbed the back of her neck and looked thought-fully out the driver's side window beyond me. "Well, I guess it depends on where you're at. If you can try to take out one of the guards while I'm talking with the wizard, then we'll only have to deal with the wizard and the other guard. He only has two that I saw, but both of them were pretty darn scary." She looked back to me. "But whatever you do, please...please be careful. I... I don't want you to be hurt. I care about you."

I slid over in the seat and wrapped my arms around her. "It'll be okay. I know it might be tough, but we'll get through it." However, from what she said, and what I knew about these people so far, I wasn't as confident on the inside as I showed her. I wanted to comfort her, but I was secretly scared that something might happen to one or both of us if we weren't careful.

Morgana nodded and rested her head against my shoul-der. "I just wish I could believe that." She trailed her hand over my chest for a moment, then slid away and hopped out of the truck. She pulled off my old clothes and set them back in the truck, folding them neatly as she did. When she looked up at me, she had a faint smile on her face. "Guess we should get this done with, then."

I nodded and followed her lead. By the time I'd gotten my clothes off, she was already in raven form, and she'd strutted around the front of the truck to stand nearby. I leaned down to touch her midnight black feathers, but she lightly tapped my foot with her beak, as if in reproach.

"Yeah, yeah. I'm shifting." I shook my head at her and took a couple steps back to give myself enough room to change, and enough room between us so my coyote didn't do anything stupid in the time it took me to regain my senses after the shift.

Once I'd completed my change, I barked at her, and she threw herself into the air. I turned and let my coyote chase after her. If I had any chance of keeping up, the beast was going to be better at this than me. His instincts were more honed on the chase, even though we both knew she was not our prey.

We traveled like that for a while. Morgana's flight pattern seemed more erratic this time, likely because she was trying to figure out where she'd come from, and inspecting the surroundings from just above the trees. I was having a harder time tracking her than ever before, and my coyote snipped at me. He wanted me to fade back into the background while he took control of the situation, but I never wanted my animal to have more control of my body than I did.

My grandmother had warned me of such things, instructing me about people who had gone insane in Native American lore by turning more beast than human. They had cannibalized others because they had forgotten how to be human. She'd been my rock through learning about my new form, keeping me sane and grounded. Of course, life with her hadn't always been easy, but it'd been better than with living with my parents and siblings. She'd shown me true love, regardless of what I looked like.

Morgana slid through the trees in a descent that made me worry she'd hit a branch or tree trunk, but she deftly navigated the forest with grace. I pushed harder to keep up with her, carrying the small red duffel bag with our borrowed clothes in it, and took care to slow as she did. I wanted to keep pace with her, but not get too close in case she made any quick stops.

She shifted into human form as her feet touched the ground, and I stopped suddenly, nearly mowing her down from the high momentum I'd built up. My paws no longer hurt, probably due to my enhanced healing in my coyote form.

I dropped the bag and joined her in human form.

"Ready for this?" she asked, worrying her lower lip. I could definitely relate to her anxiety.

"Let's get this over with." I gave her a quick kiss, then dropped down to the bag to get our clothes out. We dressed quickly, made a few last-minute plans with our new knowledge of the building's layout, then we parted ways.

I only hoped I'd be able to keep with it and take out the guard she'd mentioned without making too much noise. If I didn't get to him before he shouted his alarm, then we might be screwed. Particularly since they had us outgunned. From the wreck they'd made of her home, I didn't doubt their capabilities.

24

MORGANA

s I walked to the front door, I felt my shoulders slouch further forward. I rolled them back a time or two, easing some of the radiating tension. My nerves were fraying, but I had to keep calm, and stay on track with what I knew we were doing. It'd be fine. It really would, right? I shook the negativity from me, and knocked.

No one answered for the longest time, and I almost wondered if I'd come to the wrong cabin. They did look pretty similar. I glanced around, catching a few familiar sights. Then again, I'd been pretty dazed when I'd been here, and when I'd left.

The door opened behind me, and I nearly jumped out of my skin. The man—Jasper, I thought—leaned against the doorframe, staring at me intently.

"So, you did as you said you would, eh?" He looked up at the sun, which was out in force. It was probably two o'clock in the afternoon now. I didn't have a watch, since I was always afraid I'd lose it when I needed to shift forms quickly. Sometimes I carried one when I was with big clients, but it was more an accessory than a staple of my wardrobe.

"Quicker than I'd guessed you would be. Not bad, girlie." He reached out to grab my shoulder, but I ducked out of the way. "Stop that shit. Get inside, so we can pay you for your trouble."

"Why can't you just pay me here?" I looked inside the house, but the windows were all covered in dark blackout curtains, and my eyes were used to the sun outside, not the darker room. I couldn't see what they had in store for me.

"Because we don't like to do business on the doorstep. Now, come on." He grabbed me this time since I'd been too busy trying to focus inside. He squeezed my upper arm hard enough that I thought it might bruise later, and I bit back a cry. In the distance, I thought I heard a soft growl, but Jasper didn't seem to have heard it.

I looked back out the door a moment before he closed it in my face, but I didn't see Cody. Maybe it had just been the wind, but I kind of doubted it. I'd heard his growl a few times now, and... My heart pounded in my chest. All thoughts were cut off when I caught sight of Kevin. His face was bloody, his mouth gagged, and he was tied to a sturdy-looking chair. When he saw me, he let out a soft whimper.

I tried to jerk away from Jasper to go to Kevin, but he held onto me too hard. Even if I tried to fight him, he wouldn't let me go. "What did you do to him?" My throat tightened, and I struggled for a little bit longer, until I realized it just wasn't going to happen.

"We did what we had to do to get information out of him. You know how that goes, right?" Jasper chuckled, and he shoved me down to the floor. I grunted from the impact, and he pulled my hands behind my back, pressed his knee into my spine, and tied my hands. I jerked and wriggled again. I'd learned a few lessons when it came to making people struggle to tie you up, things that had worked before.

When they couldn't tie you their best, they made mistakes. Mistakes meant more slack, which meant an easier time slipping from them later.

What I hadn't intended was for Jasper to smack me in the back of the head with his fist. Darkness dimmed my vision for a few moments, and I sunk into unconsciousness. When I woke up again, what seemed like only minutes later, McGuire and Jasper were in the room. They were paying attention to Kevin, and not really bothering me.

"Well now Kevin, tell us—do you have enough magic to use the talisman? Don't you want to save yourself and your little girlfriend here? Don't make me think you're useless. I hate uselessness. Useless things are of no consequence, and to be honest, right now I don't feel charitable enough to keep you alive, unless you can do something for me. It's simple. Just use the talisman, and get free," McGuire taunted Kevin as he paced back and forth in front of him.

I could hear the eager breaths of Jasper close by. It seemed that he was enjoying the situation, maybe a bit too much. I felt my hands and tried to move softly. Jasper had tied my hands so tightly that my blood could barely circulate. The knots were pressed into my joints, digging into my skin. I ran a finger over them tentatively, feeling how much room I'd have available. Slowly, I began working on the ties. To a normal human, they were too tight to budge. To tie someone up properly is a matter of countering movements and the effort to undo them. The ties Jasper had made were tight and straightforward. They merely restricted my movements, trying to keep my muscles from shifting. A sharp jab to one side nearly broke the skin as the cords dug further into my arm, but I managed to get a section of my wrist lose.

Kevin's eyes darted to me for a moment before returning to the angry wizard in front of him. "Maybe you should've thought about that before beginning to torture me. Right now, I can barely stay awake. You know how the magic works, do it yourself. I know what happens when wizards are pushed too far, and I'd rather not explode in this chair," he said, trying to keep his voice confident.

McGuire pointed at me over his shoulder. "Well, maybe if we beat her up a little, it'll change your mind." The words clearly had an impact on Kevin. A look of resentment crossed his features as he slowly nodded his head.

"Fine, asshole. Give it to me," Kevin said, sounding defeated. The wizard handed him the talisman, and the effect was something I hadn't expected. A smell of tribal magic filled the cabin, and Kevin was knocked backwards against the wall. His eyes glazed over, and I bit my lip to stop myself from crying out his name.

A chuckle came from McGuire. "And that's why I'm not the first one to try things out, Morgana. I believe you brought me the wrong thing. That means one of two things: either you betrayed me and gave me the wrong object on purpose, or you got the wrong talisman. Somehow, a woman of your skills, I think you betrayed me. Jasper, get rid of her. We'll find it on our own."

With just one wrist free, I couldn't resist as Jasper pulled me up from the floor and dragged me outside. A truck pulled up as I was dragged along the ground around the building. "Hey Jasper, he got what he wanted?" Rudy yelled from the open window.

"Not yet. It's up to us," Jasper replied without stopping.

It hit me then. Regardless of what talisman I'd given them, they still intended to hurt me. The constant friction from the dirt had dragged the cords from my loosened left wrist upward, allowing me limited motion on that hand, but it didn't help me much as Jasper pushed me firmly against a tree trunk in the back.

"Now, take it like a nice little lady, and you won't hurt so much." A darkly charming smile played on his lips. It promised false hope, but I didn't fall for it, and spat on the ground. "Have it your way," he said, and backhanded me.

It felt like a truck had hit me. My vision swam for a few moments. I didn't know how much more I'd be able to take.

From the front of the house, a surprised, high-pitched noise came before it was cut off quickly. Jasper didn't notice. He brought his leg up for a kick.

I tossed my weight to the right, pulling myself away from the tree. The kick connected with the tree with a mighty thump, but I'd dodged it in time. The force of it probably would have cracked my ribs. A thud came from the yard, gaining Jasper's attention. He turned and yelled for his friend.

The impact had dislocated my right shoulder, and I writhed on the ground, slowly able to move the loops of cords enough to bring my hands in front of me. Jasper was quicker than I'd anticipated, though. He charged me as soon as he caught me breaking free, grabbing my hands and lifting me from the ground. "Pathetic. It's going to hurt now, stupid," he said and punched me with his right hand.

He kept punching me. I tried to keep my muscles pulled taut to keep him from doing permanent damage, but if I stayed at his mercy for too much longer, I was going to die.

Something was moving gravel along the side of the building, and Jasper turned his face to take a glimpse of what it was. When he was distracted, I flung myself upward on his grip and bit down on his ear. I'd aimed for the neck, but it was difficult to focus. The taste of blood filled my mouth as Jasper yelled out in pain. He threw me aside, holding his torn ear against his head.

"You bitch!" he yelled, and ran toward me. Calmly, I stared at the oncoming charge. Taking a quick two steps forward, I let my weight slink down against the dirt, and hoped that he was too dedicated in his charge to notice. Before Jasper could slow his movement, he stumbled against my leg, and rolled on the dirt.

Knowing I didn't have much time, I ran toward the front of the house, hoping to make my escape from the charging sadist behind me.

25

CODY

I saw how the big guy had manhandled Morgana into the building, and couldn't help but growl. The man's eyes never darted toward me to answer my challenge, and I let out a sigh of relief. I couldn't be exposed, not yet. My coyote slowly slunk against the dirt of the forest floor, and I made my way toward the building, taking my time. I could hear a discussion inside about using the talisman. I didn't hear Morgana, but I could easily pick out the tension. An argument built up inside the building, followed by the buffeting winds of the talisman being activated.

The clean air of the forest was quickly complemented by the smell of tribal magic from inside the cabin. I only hoped that the wizard had activated the talisman on himself. I made my way along the side of the building toward the front, in hopes of getting a peek at what was going on in the cabin, and someone big almost walked into me, dragging Morgana with him. Sinking to my back legs, I let him go by the door to the other side of the building, before peeking around. I spared a glance inside the building, to see a man staring down at Kevin, who was tied to a chair. He looked nothing like his picture after the way they'd tortured him, but his features were still identifiable.

Picking up the sounds of an approaching engine, I shied away from the door and waited to pounce on whoever was arriving. Soon, a truck made its way up to the cabin. The man inside seemed familiar with the big guy dragging Morgana with him to the side of the building.

"He got what he wanted?" the guy yelled, trying to get his voice over the sound of the idling engine. Before even hearing a reply, the man shifted in his seat, moving around a rifle and some groceries inside the cab. My attention was focused on the gun. This upped their game again, and my coyote was uneasy about them carrying a rifle into the building.

They wouldn't have it for long. I jogged around the small clearing, behind the truck.

The man inside the vehicle was struggling to get every-thing moved at once, his attention focused down on the seat next to him. I waited a few minutes to be sure he hadn't seen me, as he picked everything and headed toward the cabin. The moment the door closed, I jogged behind him. A few moments later, we were in a blind spot from the cabin's doorway, and I decided to make my move.

I bit down into his ankle. My sharp teeth sliced the leather boots he wore, and I felt a hot stream of blood on my tongue. There was a surprised, muffled cry as he fell face-first toward the dirt. Not wanting him to recover and alert his friends, I let go of the ankle and walked onto his back. My weight was enough to press him lower in the ground, and I heard him whimper as I let out a satisfied growl.

I felt his muscles tense below me, trying to catch a breath. Timing myself, I pushed down just as he heaved a breath, before lunging against his throat. The cry he'd been building up was stifled. Instead, the only sound he managed was gurgling as the life bled from him, his vocal cords and throat now a bloody ruin.

I dragged his bleeding corpse next to the house, hoping that the pooling blood wouldn't be too obvious. Now, with him out of the way, I needed to find Morgana. Turning to the side of the building, I saw a huge man repeatedly beating her, holding her by the wrists. I thought about just running for her, but this man seemed different. There was something off about him that made me wary. If I just ran at him, there was a chance he'd snap her neck, killing her instantly. No, I needed her to get away first.

I walked into a small opening in the back, intended to hold the house's trashcan. After snooping for a few seconds, I found a can of soda on the ground and bit into it softly. The *crunch* of aluminum distracted from the sound of Morgana being beaten, and a loud thump as something was thrown.

I could hear the man cursing and calling Morgana names, before I heard her footsteps retreating from the tree line toward the house. Soon, something massive followed. The man was doing a full head-on charge at Morgana, and I decided to act. I was happy to have such soft pads in my paws as I ran to close the gap between us. Where he made a huge racket, my running was barely audible. With a final push, I shoved my fangs along his falling leg and dug into the joints of his ankle.

There was a surprised yell, but the man barely punched me off, ignoring the gash my teeth opened up as my fangs were forcibly removed from his leg. The punch had been a strong one, but it connected at an off angle. If it had hit me full-force, I would've blacked out. Whatever he was, he definitely wasn't human. The blood on my tongue from his wounds tasted like an animal instead, like that of another shifter.

I pulled myself up from the ground in time to see the man's knee heading for my nose. "Don't meddle. You'll pay the price for interfering," he said as it connected with my face.

The back of my head snapped toward the right, and instead of fighting it, I rolled with it. My left side slid on the dirt as I hit the ground. I knew I was in shock. The end of my muzzle was bloodied, and I felt like I was missing a few teeth at the front. My tongue had barely missed being serrated inside my mouth. Assessing the damage, I realized the entire length of my nose was numb. I just hoped there wasn't a fracture.

I tried opening my mouth, but to my horror, my jaws barely moved enough to let me pant. Dizzily, I took a tentative step up and saw the man preparing to charge at me. I didn't think I could take the full force of his impact. I had to move.

Pushing my weight up hurt, and I knew there were a number of bruises building, but those could be ignored. For humans, pain was there to prevent you from hurting yourself further. Shifters typically healed faster, and from nearly any kind of abuse our bodies took on a regular basis. To us, pain was an annoyance, just something to push through.

The man had built up his charge and took off at me. My coyote grinned. He was strong, but we were quicker. If I couldn't overpower him, then I'd outmaneuver him. Pushing my abused body to the edge, I prepared for the inevitable torture I'd make my legs take. Time seemed to slow down as I focused on his muscles bulging, giving me a tell when he was fully committed to it. There—a small change in angle on his right foot. I patiently waited for him to begin the swivel-like motion that would end only one way, a massive kick that would carry his full momentum to a deadly impact.

To his surprise, suddenly I was no longer on the ground. My back legs were screaming from the push, but it was worth it. My jaw could barely open, but my paws weren't useless. As I jumped over him, I let them scratch against his face. The long claws in my abused back legs bought purchase off his skin, and I could feel him howl beneath me, even before his charge had come to an end.

My coyote wanted to let out its satisfaction for having outsmarted the opponent, but I knew it was a trick that would only work once. The man turned to me, and I saw the damage to his face. Long scratches ran from the top of his forehead down to his jawline. I'd barely missed his eyes, but the deep gashes were bleeding massively. For a human that would be a thing of concern, but he just shrugged and took slow, deliberate steps toward me.

A loud shot came from somewhere to my right, and I saw a surprise in the man's face as an opening started to form in middle of his chest. Behind me, Morgana yelled something that I had a hard time focusing on. My attention was on my opponent, who slowly tumbled to the ground. The round had struck true to his heart. She must have found the rifle and come to my aid.

To be safe, I jogged over to him and made sure he was dead. Since my fangs were useless, I decided to change back to a human. The process was painful, since shifting helped accelerate my healing. When I was done, I was spent. The impact that had hurt slightly on my nose as a coyote, now throbbed painfully against the entire side of my face. Hair-line fractures most likely crisscrossed my skull, but at least I was still alive.

She came to support me as I recovered. Inside the cabin, I heard a yell of frustration. "Get out of here," I said weakly, looking into Morgana's eyes. She had to get out before the wizard came out. I doubted either one of us was up for a fight with him.

There was a change in her eyes, a steeling of her will. "No. Not this time," Morgana said gently and turned toward the opening of the cabin. I tried to drag myself upright, but before I had a chance, the wizard was on us.

A jolt of lightning hit Morgana and branched off to me as the wizard made his way toward us. "You killed my pet," he yelled as he threw another bolt at us. The convulsions were bad, making us arch into shapes not intended for human form. My muscles and nerves were on fire as the current ran through us. Unable to scream, I waited for the pain to end. My coyote was focused on survival, dragging us slowly along the dirt toward the edge of the forest.

"See, Morgana, he's crawling away from you. All of your friends are abandoning you, or they're already dead. That pathetic boy in the chair back there, this guy here, and everyone else," he taunted between casting his spells.

"Kevin!" Morgana yelled as the tied-up man from inside the cabin turned the corner, looking barely conscious of what was going on.

The wizard slammed us all with an invisible wall of force, throwing us around the yard. "You will all suffer," he muttered as he began to chant something different. The air around him seemed to thicken, and judging by Kevin's reaction, whatever he was casting now would make everything before it seem insignificant.

I was dragging myself backward, trying to get my muscles to function, when my hands touched my bag of clothes. I turned around and tore it open, looking for the talisman within. Whatever it would cause should at least distract the wizard. I needed some more time, though— Morgana had said that it took time for the talisman to work its magic.

I pulled it against my chest, ignoring the fact that it was covered in my blood, and began to chant quietly. It was one of the older chants my grandmother shared with everyone as they were growing up. It was a child's chant for protection, and a plea for help from the spirits.

Out in the yard, I saw Kevin drag himself upward from the ground and throw a ball of white energy at the wizard. McGuire laughed as the ball of energy simply fused with his body. "You got to do more than that, kid." He lashed out at Kevin and Morgana with black tendrils of energy. I'd never heard anyone scream the way they did. The tendrils burrowed inside their skin and danced underneath, pulling on every vein and strand of muscle.

I could suddenly smell the tribal magic building up, and I knew that the wizard had detected it too. "Ha! That's where you have it. Don't worry, I'll kill you soon enough." He began to walk my way, releasing Morgana and Kevin from the tendrils and turning them toward me instead as he walked closer. The scent of rotting meat rolled off him in waves. The closer he got, the stronger the smell became. I closed my eyes, focusing on the chant and keeping the talisman safe from him.

A sudden yell of surprise came from in front of me and I allowed myself to steal a glance at what was going on. Kevin had thrown a rock at the wizard, and it seemed to have distracted him, making him turn around. With a flick of a wrist, the wizard sent his tendrils out toward Kevin again.

Before they connected, I felt the talisman vibrate in my hands. "You want power so much? Here!" I yelled, and singled out McGuire in my mind. Without a lot of effort, I felt the talisman begin its magic.

The tendrils waned midair and began to retract toward the wizard. An ululating cry came from his lips as the outer edge of his skin began changing: first into blackened, rotting meat, and then into pure gold. Slowly the change took him over, layer by layer, until he was merely a terrifyingly realistic gold statue.

26

CODY

My body ached from the fight, but we'd made it out alive. I placed my arm under Morgana's shoulder, supporting her as she limped from the cabin. Whatever bruises she'd had before were nothing to what she sported now. We both looked like we'd been doing some serious cage fighting. With my other arm, I helped Kevin who nearly tripped and fell on his face when he finally got to his feet. He looked dazed and completely out of it.

If I'd been thinking more clearly, I would've taken my grandmother's truck here, because now we had to walk her friend and ourselves back to her home. It was the closest place that we could go. But the downside of bringing the truck would've been finding a place to park it, and potentially letting people know we were there, which would've put us at even more of a disadvantage. While we could've taken the bad guys' truck, we would've drawn more attention to ourselves than necessary. This was safer.

The walk took quite a while, and by the time we were done, all of us had managed to fall to the forest floor a few times and acquire new bruises, cuts, and scrapes. Time had morphed and become a fantastical thing. It no longer mattered, really. The only thing that mattered was that we were safe. My feet would normally have hurt like crazy due to the massive amounts of walking we'd done in the past twenty-four hours, but right now they didn't. Probably because so many other things hurt too.

By the time we got to Morgana's house, twilight was painting the sky in brilliant hues of color, and darkness was setting in. The more I looked at Kevin, the more I saw how out of it he was. It wouldn't be a good idea for him to go home right now, especially not on his own, which he kept muttering about.

"I'll be fine," he slurred a little. "Just need some rest. It's...okay. I've...survived...worse."

I figured he might've, but that didn't matter now. I wasn't going to just let him go off on his own. He was a friend of Morgana's, and in my estimation he wasn't in good enough shape to be alone, although I wasn't a doctor. He seemed to have burned out a little.

Morgana opened the door and invited both of us in. Instinctively I took in a deep breath, sniffing the air to determine if we were alone in the house. The air merely carried the scent of the conflict that had happened here not too long ago, with no sign of anyone having been here since. "Hey, Morgana. You think maybe Kevin might need some sleep?" I finally voiced my concern about him openly.

"There really isn't any place for him to lie down on. Let's get some of this cleared out," she said, but it was too late.

Kevin had sat in a chair with a stack of papers on his lap, his head tilted backwards. The deep snores coming from his direction left no question about his state of consciousness. I guess his weariness finally managed to get the upper hand.

"We need to talk," I said softly to Morgana as I helped her move some papers and maps aside. "The talisman must be returned to my people soon, but there's a huge golden statue out there. I think it's a little too suspicious, don't you think? And I still have to find a way to pay for your services," I continued before she held up her hand to silence me.

"Well, I think I can take care of both problems at the same time. My clients are always looking for some weird things and, to be honest, a solid golden statue with its features in agony will most likely be on the wish list of some wealthy person out there. When it comes to the talisman, I've seen enough what it did, especially to your cousin. While I may not like all my clients, I'd rather have them as repeat customers than dead husks somewhere," Morgana said, pacing back and forth putting papers in correct drawers.

Somehow, I wasn't shocked. Either because knowing what kind of people had needs for her services had made me more open to the idea that almost anything different had a price in the black market, or because the fight had just made me so numb. And knowing her clients, they probably wanted to keep the purchase of the corpse—errr, the wizard statue—under wraps as much as possible. That left just one thing: I had to return the talisman soon.

"We've fought and gotten banged up, and I'm exhausted. But we need to keep an eye on Kevin. He seems really out of it," I spoke softly, knowing that she cared for him. Outside the forest was quiet, and heavy with the scent of impending rain.

She seemed to pick on it too, her eyes looking toward the window closest to her. "Maybe it's my turn to make sure he'll snap out of it later. I owe him at least that much," she said and returned her eyes to me.

With a nod, I turned my gaze so as not to come across challenging, or too possessive. I didn't care about my pain, but there was hurt behind her eyes that was too much to bear. I knew it would take time for her to talk in detail about what happened with Ezra, but when she was ready, I'd be there. In the meantime, we'd deal with everything one day at a time.

27

MORGANA

I stretched a little as the light from the sun caressed my cheek. I couldn't believe that I'd sleep the entire night away. I looked up to see Cody walking into the bedroom with a tray. I rubbed my eyes, only now smelling the delicious food coming from the kitchen, and frowned up at him. "You didn't have to cook."

"I don't mind." He smiled, then winced a little.

One side of his face was completely bruised, and I could tell that the shifter from McGuire's cabin had socked him pretty hard. I couldn't believe he'd managed to survive that, let alone be in the decent shape he was in otherwise. I felt like I'd been hit by a speeding train, and I hadn't even been as heavily involved in the fight as he had. I'd done what I could to help, but seeing Cody wield the talisman and turn the wizard into a statue like that had been a big deal. He'd exerted a lot of energy to do it, and still managed to bring the two of us and Kevin back to my home.

He set the tray on my lap. It was a yummy breakfast of eggs, bacon, hash browns, and toast, with a side of grapes and some apple juice. All the staples. My stomach growled just looking at it, and I picked up the fork to start digging in. I glanced at him and realized he was just watching me eat.

"Aren't you going to eat too?" I frowned.

"Already did. I was up earlier, and I probably should've waited for you, but I didn't want to wake you. After yesterday, I know you needed your rest."

A crash sounded from the living room, and I nearly jumped off the bed, but I remained still so I wouldn't spill anything. There'd already been enough things messed up in my house.

Cody placed his hand on my shoulder. "I'll go check. Kevin's still here, and he's still feeling pretty disoriented from getting beaten up. I've told him he should probably go to a doctor, but he keeps declining. Maybe you can get him to listen to you."

I let out a breath, feeling a little more comfortable knowing it was him and not McGuire, Jasper, or Rudy. For a moment, I'd wondered if maybe yesterday had all been a dream—or more likely a nightmare—but it hadn't been. I nodded. "Yeah, I can talk to him. There's a doctor in town who handles all sorts of crazy things since there's a large supernatural presence here in Woodland Creek. I'm sure I can convince him to go." I wanted to suggest that maybe he could go too, but he seemed pretty okay. Besides, the two of us were shifters, with a bit better healing rate than Kevin.

"Good. But first, finish up your breakfast. After all that shifting, and not really eating afterward to regain your strength...it's just better for you to eat right now. I want to make sure you're well on the path to recovery too." He started to smile again, but caught himself in time. I could still see the lightness in his eyes, though, and I loved that.

"I will." I sat there for a moment watching as he left the room, softly closing the door behind him. Now that the battle was behind us, where did we go from here? There wasn't anyone waiting in the wings to kill us again...yet. Did we go with it, or should we call it quits before something worse happened?

I didn't think I'd be able to ever call it quits with Cody. He meant so much more to me than I would've thought possible.

Our relationship was different than I'd ever had with anyone else. We were a team, a partnership. Ezra and I had been lovers, but we hadn't had that kind of mutual trust. I couldn't be completely sure if that's what Cody felt for me, though. I guess I'd have to talk with him about it once we got Kevin the assistance he needed.

I finished my food, savoring every bit, but didn't waste too much time. It was better to get our day started. I vaguely remembered Cody saying he wanted to give the talisman back to his grandmother for safekeeping. I thought that was the best plan. After I'd seen what it could do last night, it scared me. The pain the wizard had gone through and sheer terror in his face as he became what he'd craved so much would stick with me for a while.

Letting out a breath, I tried to recover some of my composure, and then I went out into the living room to see Kevin and Cody. I'd taken a shower and put on some fresh clothes, since I'd collapsed into bed last night with no thought at all about being hot, sweaty, and battered. The only thing on my mind had been recouping my lost energy.

I opened the door to the living room and glanced out to see Kevin lying on the couch with Cody on the armchair. They were talking a little here and there, and there was a

SARAH MÄKELÄ

half-finished plate of food on the coffee table in front of
Kevin and a mug near Cody. I thought I smelled the faint
scent of coffee, but I knew I didn't have any in the house.
Then again, I hadn't remembered having much in the way
of breakfast food either.

My heart ached, and I looked to Cody. That must've
been something for him to hit the grocery store after what
he'd been through. Both of them turned to look at me, and
Kevin waved a hand before glancing back out the window.

Cody rose to come to me, but I motioned for him to stay
put. "I'm fine. I promise." And that was the truth. I hadn't
thought I could possibly get out of bed, but after my shower,
I almost felt new again.

I came closer to them and looked between the couch,
where Kevin lay, and Cody. I wondered what they'd talked
about, and if Kevin knew that I was with Cody now. What
would he think? Would he fault me for moving on after
Ezra, even though he'd been the one to tell me that I should?
I pushed my worries aside and climbed into Cody's lap,
resting my head against his shoulder. I heard him groan
softly under me, and I started to rise, but he held me close.

"I'm fine, babe. No worries." He ran his hand over my
back in a soothing gesture, and I savored the warmth his
body exuded. My eyelids grew a little heavier. I could have
totally just fallen asleep in his arms.

Kevin just watched us. He didn't say anything, but the
look of satisfaction on his face proved my worries wrong.
Why had I ever doubted that he would approve? Maybe he
knew how self-destructive I'd been before I met Cody.

"Kevin, you really should see a doctor. I know of one in
town who'll be able to help you." I smiled at him. "He
handles supernatural patients, so you don't have to worry
about being a wizard with him."

"He's that shifter doctor, isn't he? Dr. Desmond Callahan, right?" Kevin sighed and leaned his head back against the arm of the couch. "Geez...like I told Cody, I'm fine. I really am. I just need some rest, and to make a healing potion."

The blood drained from my face at the mention of him making a potion. With his lab being as completely destroyed as it was, I didn't think he'd be able to make anything for a while. Let alone in his current shape.

He blinked at me. "I don't like that look. That look means there's something seriously wrong. What's wrong?" He sat up quickly and nearly tumbled from the couch. I hopped out of Cody's lap to stabilize Kevin. "No, not the lab."

"I'm so sorry. They broke a lot of things in there. I know how much it meant to you." I kept my hand on his shoulder, trying to be a comforting presence, but he was busy scowling.

"Damn it. That asshole. If I could, I'd bring him back to life just to kill him again." He slumped forward and put his head in his hands. "Guess I'll have to get busy. You're not going to be giving up treasure hunting, are you? Please say you aren't. That's the only way I can think of gathering the resources to rebuild."

I looked to Cody, knowing that I didn't need his input, but having his acceptance of my decision would mean a lot to me. He nodded just enough for me to see his answer.

"Yeah, I'm still a treasure hunter. It's in my blood." I pushed my shoulders back, feeling some pain shooting through them as I did so. Okay, maybe it wasn't a good idea to get cocky, especially not right now.

"For better or worse, huh?"

I grimaced. I guess he was right. But I thought of it being for better now, especially having someone at my back that I trusted. I'd be more careful now, and I'd likely at least move to a different part of town, so that whoever had given out my information wouldn't be able to share it with others again. I frowned, thinking of the one person who had it, and knew what I did. But Kevin wouldn't ever give it out, would he? I frowned at him, wondering about that. It would kind of make sense, especially if he was all about expanding his basement laboratory. He'd had all sorts of high-tech gear in there. But he'd also had all his stuff trashed too.

If he had, he'd gotten what he deserved. Once I moved, I wouldn't tell him my information again. I'd come to him only when I needed something. That's when I saw the effects of Ezra's death on him. The colder, more jaded person, who was influenced by money instead of friendship. I guess we'd each had our own faults after that. I just didn't realize before how far down he might've gone.

He frowned at me and ran a hand through his hair. He pushed up into a sitting position, not as faint as he'd been before. "Um, yeah. I'm going to head off."

"That's a good idea." I watched him hobble toward the sliding glass door.

Cody looked between us, his brows drawing together. He'd seen the exchange and was curious, but he didn't say anything just yet. When Kevin had closed the door and was walking off toward the woods through the glass, Cody came to sit beside me. "You're thinking he had something to do with this?"

"I don't think he did directly, but I keep my personal information safe. I take my clients through a private email address. That's why I was surprised when I saw you on my doorstep and when I received the call from James McGuire." I placed my hand on his thigh, then looked up into his eyes. "How did you know to come here?"

"One of my professors gave me the email address of some wiz... Damn it." He shook his head. "I should've told you sooner, but I was so hell-bent on getting the talisman back for my family—and claiming a spot in your life—that I didn't think about how easy it had been to get your location."

I leaned into him. "It's not your fault. I probably should've questioned this sooner, but now that you're in my life, I guess I'll have moving help." I grinned up at him mischievously.

"Just using me for my muscles," he said, a smile brightening his eyes. "I guess that'll work so long as you let me crash at your place occasionally. My roommate at the dorm likes watching TV until the wee hours, and keeps me awake."

"Who's to say I wouldn't keep you up late too?" I winked at him, and the humor in his gaze was replaced with something more primal and dangerous.

"I think I'd take that kind of staying awake over listening to him watching cartoons." He pulled me closer, careful to not hurt me. "Maybe I'd like another sample of how you'd be keeping me up." A smoldering grin spread across his lips.

Moisture pooled between my legs from that look, as well as the feel of his warm body beside me. *Oh, boy...* He scooped me into his arms and carried me to the bedroom, kicking the door shut behind us.

Cody crossed the room in a few long strides, then set me onto the bed. He leaned into me pressing me down into the mattress. I loved the feeling of him over me like this. None of the aches and pain from yesterday mattered right now, only being here with him.

I slid my hands to the hem of his shirt, enjoying the

flexing of his rock-hard abs beneath it. Our lips met in a sensual brush of passion, but the kiss didn't remain like that for long. It grew into something more like a torrential storm following a gentle breeze.

We removed one another's clothes, tossing them to the floor. Somehow I doubted we'd been needing them again soon. His naked body was all hard, delicious muscle. My gaze trailed down to his large cock, and my mouth went a little dry. The idea of him filling me made my core clench.

I circled my legs around his waist to pull him closer. His nostrils twitched, and he grinned at me, probably knowing just how badly I wanted this. "I don't think I have to ask if you want this."

"You better not." My voice was husky, almost sounding foreign to my own ears. Cody brought out a different, wilder side of me that I wanted to explore with him for the rest of our days.

He ran a hand over my breast, kneading it lightly before swiping his thumb over the hardened nipple. Arousal spread in the pit of my stomach, and I bit back a moan. He dipped his head to take the other nipple into his mouth. This time, I couldn't stop my cry of pleasure.

I angled my hips toward his and pushed against him, causing him to slide against my clit. I rocked my hips against his cock. *Two can play this game.*

A low groan rumbled in his chest, and he pulled away to put on a condom. The last thing we needed to worry about was little ravens or coyotes prowling around. He slid between my legs again. This time when I pushed against him, his tip slid inside me. Ecstasy swept through my body.

He grabbed my legs, holding them in the crook of his elbows. His fingers dug into my thighs as he pushed farther inside me. When he was all the way in, he paused for a moment, letting me get accustomed to his thick shaft.

I couldn't wait though. My body was burning for him at a fever pitch. This needed to happen. He couldn't draw this out. Both of us knew it. His body vibrated with lust between my legs. I thrust against him, taking the initiative. He leaned back his head, and I watched his Adam's apple bob. When he looked back at me, his eyes were golden, like a coyote's instead of the blue that had drawn me to him.

His hips met my thrusts at first, but that didn't last long. He slammed into me over and over, so hard I could only wrap my arms around his neck and my legs around his waist, and endure the sweet blend of heady desire he stirred in me.

I pulled him near again, nibbling his throat and running my mouth along his jawline before settling on his lips. "God, Cody, you're amazing," I murmured. Our tongues entwined in their own rhythmic dance as our climax grew ever closer to overtaking us.

Cody's steady pace grew more out of control. Knowing he was as far gone as I was threw me over the edge. I squeezed my eyes closed and screamed as pleasure crashed into me. My body convulsed at the sheer intensity. The tight squeeze of Cody's hands on my thighs and his guttural growl of release were the only things keeping me anchored.

My breath came out in ragged pants as I opened my eyes. He pulled away enough to drop onto the bed beside me. "I'm glad I picked up some frozen pizza while I was out now. I need more of that," he said.

I ran a hand through his hair, smiling at him. "You and me both."

Loneliness and regret were a thing of the past. If there was one thing that Kevin had done right, it was convincing me to move on. Now I had Cody, and I knew that life would be better because I'd stepped out from the shadow of grief to give him a chance. Our path might not be easy, but to have his love and him in my life, it would certainly be worth having him on the journey too.

———

In the mood for more shapeshifters? Grab *Beneath the Broken Moon: Season One...*

AUTHOR'S NOTE

Thank you for reading *Moonlit Feathers*. I hope you enjoyed it!

Please consider leaving a review at the retailer's website or on Goodreads, even if it's a line or two. It truly helps!

For more books from the Woodland Creek series, visit: https://woodlandcreekseries.com/

If you're interested in being the first to know about my next release, sign up for my newsletter.

ABOUT THE AUTHOR

New York Times & USA Today Bestselling Author Sarah Mäkelä loves her fiction dark, magical, and passionate. She is a paranormal romance author and a life-long paranormal fan who still sleeps with a night light. In her spare time, she reads sexy books, watches scary movies, and plays computer games with her husband. When she gets the chance, she loves traveling the world too.

amazon.com/author/sarahmakela

bookbub.com/authors/sarah-makela

instagram.com/authorsarahmakela

facebook.com/authorsarahmakela

twitter.com/sarahmakela

goodreads.com/sarahmakela

pinterest.com/authorsarahmakela

ALSO BY SARAH MÄKELÄ

Currently Available for Free *

Cry Wolf Series

(New Adult Paranormal Romance)

Book 1: The Witch Who Cried Wolf *

Book 2: Cold Moon Rising

Book 3: The Wolf Who Played With Fire

Book 4: Highland Moon Rising

Book 5: The Selkie Who Loved A Wolf

Book 6: The Leopard Who Claimed A Wolf

Cry Wolf Series Boxed Set (Books 1-3)

Beneath the Broken Moon Serial

(New Adult Paranormal Romance)

Part 1 *

Part 2

Part 3

Part 4

Part 5

Season One (Parts 1-5)

Edge of Oblivion

Book 1: The Assassin's Mark

Book 2: The Thief's Gambit

The Amazon Chronicles Series

(New Adult Paranormal Romance)

Book 1: Jungle Heat

Book 2: Jungle Fire

Book 3: Jungle Blaze

Book 4: Jungle Burn

The Amazon Chronicles Collection

Hacked Investigations Series

(Futuristic Paranormal Romance)

Book 1: Techno Crazed

Book 2: Savage Bytes

Book 2.5: Internet Dating for Gnomes *

Book 3: Blacklist Rogue

Book 4: Digital Slave

Courts of Light and Dark

(New Adult Fantasy Romance)

Book 1: Captivated

Book 2: Surrendered

Standalones

Moonlit Feathers

Captive Moonlight

Vera's Christmas Elf

EXCERPT FOR BENEATH THE BROKEN MOON: PART TWO

DEREK

The headcount began, signaling the start of the High Council meeting. I reclined in a plush red velvet chair next to Elliot, already wanting it to be over with. Many years ago, the meetings had appealed to me, and I'd listened to the drawn-out political babbling as if it all mattered. Now I forced myself to attend.

Sadly, that wasn't the only thing worrying me. Someone was after me, and I didn't know who or why. What did they know about me? If someone had discovered I helped Carmela... I locked the thought away. Some vampires were telepathic; thinking of her could be treacherous.

The other council members were from all walks of life, and ranged in appearance from young adult to elder. Some smelled as if they'd walked in from a shantytown, while others were well-groomed and polished.

A few kept their minor nocturne minions seated at their feet in what the council believed was a manner appropriate to their class. I didn't subscribe to that school of thought. Who was becoming extinct? Nocturnes. Who was the threat? The humans striving to build up their numbers again.

The progress humans and nocturnes alike had made over the centuries had mostly been lost, secreted away by the human government in their laboratories and military bases. They thought their wealth could protect them from the horrors of this new post-apocalyptic life, but history had proven time and again that the average person wouldn't be suppressed forever.

Lord Prescott entered from his private chambers at the front of the room. He appeared young and lanky, as if he was in his late teens or early twenties, but he'd been the High Council's chairman for centuries before I was even born. The power emanating from him swept through the chamber, flooding everyone with its intensity.

Goosebumps pricked my flesh, and I clenched the arms of my chair. Elliot stiffened beside me. One would think we'd get used to this after a while, but Prescott made sure his vampires obeyed him. No one would dare to threaten his position.

"Most of you know why we've gathered here." Prescott stood next to his throne. He fixed his gaze on me. "Why don't you remind us, Derek Ashmoore. I'm sure you know, yes?"

My lips pulled away from my fangs, but I forced my expression to remain neutral. Giving him a piece of my mind wouldn't be best. "As the chairman, I assumed you would tell everyone why we're here."

Prescott narrowed his grey eyes at me, then turned to another vampire. "Giles Cleaver, what's the main item on our agenda?"

Giles, a crooked old vampire, cast a haughty glance my way before addressing Prescott and everyone else. "We are here to acknowledge the death of Tom Turner, a senior High Council member. You shall pick the newest senior member, my lord." He bowed at the waist before sitting back down.

"You received the memo. Good." Prescott seated himself on the throne. "As Giles said, one of our own has been murdered. This doesn't even speak to the fact that the kindred beneath us are murdered every day by those human creatures. The *Cazador*... what a dreadful name." He entwined his fingers over his flat stomach and observed the council members.

"Who is worthy of fulfilling the role of senior member? Who has earned his place among us and will act in our best interests?" He narrowed his gaze on me, and the muscles in my shoulders tensed. Prescott swiped his tongue across his slightly yellowed fangs, enjoying the sight of watching me squirm; then he twisted his attention to my right.

"Elliot Quinn. How long have you been among us? Since the reign of Queen Victoria, yes?"

Elliot stood with his head bowed. "No, my lord, I became a vampire during King Edward VII's reign." His knuckles were white from clenching his hands together.

"Yes, that's right. Still, you have a few centuries under your belt, and continue to prove yourself useful." Prescott scanned the room, drawing out the spectacle.

Elliot retook his seat after a few moments. He nearly vibrated with nervous energy, which wasn't like him at all. This was a big deal for him, since he still believed we could make a difference through politics.

I leaned forward in my chair, resting my hands on my knees. Prescott needed to pick someone already, and end this verbose meeting. One of our kind had been killed, and that led me to wonder if the attacks on me were related.

What reason would a necromancer have for putting his

life on the line to kidnap vampires, though? Maybe Tom's death wasn't connected.

"Head in the clouds today, Derek?" Prescott steepled his fingers under his chin. He shot a tidal wave of power at me, hitting me in the chest. My body jerked back into the chair at the impact, and the air rushed from my lungs. Agony burned inside me like a blazing torch. I clenched my hands into fists to keep from reacting. "See me after the meeting. Now, focus on our business here."

I flinched, no longer wanting to be here. Elliot bumped my foot. No, this wasn't the way to get on Prescott's good side after my absence.

"At any rate, I will promote Elliot Quinn as the newest senior High Council member. As far as Tom Turner's death, I *will* find who committed this crime. If I find anyone to be less than honest and forthright with information, I will rid this forsaken planet of you and your underlings. Obey our laws, and don't bring harm upon our kindred. We need to remain strong. Understood?"

A low rumbling of agreement filled the air.

"Good. If no one has any further concerns, we will adjourn."

The room remained silent.

Council members very rarely offered up their fears to Prescott in the public forum. Most tried to stay out of the spotlight.

"Adjourned." Prescott rose from his chair with flourish, brushing aside his platinum blond hair, and waited there.

"What was that about?" Elliot whispered as we walked down the stairs of the large lecture hall. A couple of vampires shook their heads at me as they filed toward the exit.

"Derek, come. Let's go to my office." Prescott waved his

hand toward the door of the private chambers near his throne. "Elliot, you may join us if you wish."

I cut my gaze to Elliot. He should go home instead of getting wrapped up in this.

Something was wrong; I could sense it the closer I got to Prescott. He masked how he truly felt in public behind a façade, but I'd spent enough time with him over the centuries to pick up on his mannerisms.

We followed him into his grand office. Many Renaissance paintings lined the walls, and a colossal crystal chandelier hung overhead. I kept my arms at my sides, focusing on remaining calm and neutral, especially after my misbehavior during the meeting. Besides, Elliot had warned me about Prescott being on edge due to my recent lapse in attendance.

Our chairman sat in a massive brown leather chair behind his ornate mahogany desk, and waved to the crimson seats facing it.

Elliot took the one on the right, and I sat in the other.

"Congratulations on your promotion, Elliot. You are witness to this discussion." My friend nodded, and Prescott turned his gaze on me. "What distracted you in the chamber? You don't like politics, but there is an air of unease about you. You *will* tell me the truth."

Thankfully, Prescott wasn't a telepath, but he was excellent at deciphering lies.

I lowered my head. "I'm wary after hearing about Tom Turner, my lord. An attack was made on my life yesterday." It took all my strength not to shift in my chair, especially under Prescott's watchful eyes.

He nodded. "I see. You clearly fought off your assailants. Did you know either of them?"

I shook my head. "I did not."

"If I may, my lord..." Elliot stood and bowed at the waist.

Prescott waved his hand in dismissal. "Save the formalities for the council's chamber."

"I visited Derek at his home and noticed a familiar scent, presumably belonging to one of the attackers."

"And who would that be? Do you have more than that? A name, perhaps?" Prescott turned the full weight of his gaze on Elliot.

"Sadly, I don't recall where I know the scent from." Elliot didn't shrink back.

"Disappointing." Prescott examined a few papers on his desk. "I'd need more information before I can say if the attacks are connected." He leaned back in his chair, glancing between us. "I have the initial information on Tom's death here. If you agree not to speak of this matter with anyone else, I will share it with you."

"I won't say anything." If my attempted kidnapping was connected, I might figure out who was after me. I doubted whoever it was would give up so easily.